Praise

the Blood Coven

"You'll get bitten and love it."

—Rachel Caine, *New York Times* bestselling author

Night School

"An action-packed story with appealing characters, dark humor, and a new spin on both the worlds of the undead and the fae. Though primarily targeted to a YA audience, this novel will appeal to adult fans of *Buffy the Vampire Slayer* as well as the Harry Potter series and the Twilight novels."

—*Library Journal*

"Another thrilling installment to Rayne and Sunny's story!"

—*Romance Reviews Today*

"Fifth of the Blood Coven Vampire series takes a darker turn . . . [an] engaging young adult urban fantasy. It is entertaining watching the twins mature through this fast-paced series that packs enough twists and humor to hold readers' attention to the last page."   —*Monsters and Critics*

"This book has it all! Vampires, vampire slayers, and faeries, what more could you ask for? . . . a fast-paced book from start to finish. I can't wait to read more about Sunny and Rayne's adventures. This is a must read for anyone who enjoys paranormal fiction and a good story."

—*Night Owl Reviews*

continued . . .

Bad Blood

"A vampire book so worth reading, with dark humor, distinctive voice, and a protagonist clever enough to get herself out of trouble . . . A great ride."

—Ellen Hopkins,
New York Times bestselling author

"Mancusi writes with a wicked sense of humor and keeps readers turning the pages, eager for more."

—*Novel Reads*

Girls That Growl

"An amusing teenage vampire tale starring a fascinating high school student . . . Young adults will enjoy growling alongside of this vampire slayer who has no time left for homework."

—*Midwest Book Review*

"A fast-paced and entertaining read."   —*Love Vampires*

"A refreshing new vampire story, *Girls That Growl* is different from all of those other vampire stories . . . a very original plot."

—*Flamingnet*

Stake That

"A fast-paced story line . . . both humorous and hip . . . A top read!"
—*Love Vampires*

"Rayne is a fascinating protagonist . . . readers will want to stake out Mari Mancusi's fun homage to Buffy."
—*The Best Reviews*

Boys That Bite

"A wonderfully original blend of vampire/love/adventure drama which teens will find refreshingly different."
—*Midwest Book Review*

"Liberal doses of humor keep things interesting . . . and the surprise ending will leave readers bloodthirsty for the next installment of the twins' misadventures with the undead. A ghoulishly fun read."
—*School Library Journal*

"A tongue-in-cheek young teen tale starring two distinct, likable twins, the vampire between them, and a coven of terrific support characters who bring humor and suspense to the mix . . . Filled with humor and action . . . insightfully fun."
—*The Best Reviews*

Blood Forever

MARI MANCUSI

BERKLEY BOOKS, NEW YORK

THE BERKLEY PUBLISHING GROUP
Published by the Penguin Group
Penguin Group (USA) Inc.
375 Hudson Street, New York, New York 10014, USA
Penguin Group (Canada), 90 Eglinton Avenue East, Suite 700, Toronto, Ontario M4P 2Y3, Canada
(a division of Pearson Penguin Canada Inc.) • Penguin Books Ltd., 80 Strand, London WC2R 0RL,
England • Penguin Group Ireland, 25 St. Stephen's Green, Dublin 2, Ireland (a division of Penguin
Books Ltd.) • Penguin Group (Australia), 250 Camberwell Road, Camberwell, Victoria 3124, Australia
(a division of Pearson Australia Group Pty. Ltd.) • Penguin Books India Pvt. Ltd., 11 Community
Centre, Panchsheel Park, New Delhi—110 017, India • Penguin Group (NZ), 67 Apollo Drive,
Rosedale, Auckland 0632, New Zealand (a division of Pearson New Zealand Ltd.) • Penguin Books
(South Africa) (Pty.) Ltd., 24 Sturdee Avenue, Rosebank, Johannesburg 2196, South Africa

Penguin Books Ltd., Registered Offices: 80 Strand, London WC2R 0RL, England

This book is an original publication of The Berkley Publishing Group.

This is a work of fiction. Names, characters, places, and incidents either are the product of the author's
imagination or are used fictitiously, and any resemblance to actual persons, living or dead, business
establishments, events, or locales is entirely coincidental. The publisher does not have any control over
and does not assume any responsibility for author or third-party websites or their content.

PUBLISHING HISTORY
Berkley trade paperback edition / September 2012

Library of Congress Cataloging-in-Publication Data

Mancusi, Marianne.
Blood forever : a Blood Coven vampires novel / by Mari Mancusi. — Berkley trade pbk. ed.
p.   cm.
Summary: After making a deal with the devil, Rayne and her twin sister Sunny
have been given the chance to go back in time to prevent that fateful night
when Sunny was bitten by vampire Magnus from ever happening.
ISBN 978-0-425-25303-8 (pbk.)
[1. Vampires—Fiction.   2. Twins—Fiction.   3. Sisters—Fiction.   4. Time travel—Fiction.]   I. Title.
PZ7.M312178Blo   2012
[Fic]—dc23   2012011766

PRINTED IN THE UNITED STATES OF AMERICA

10 9 8 7 6 5 4 3 2 1

ALWAYS LEARNING   PEARSON

To my wonderful readers. I couldn't do this without your support and encouragement. And to Jacob, the most supportive husband imaginable—thanks for all the dinners on deadline days. And to baby Avalon— this is the first book I've written with you in my life. When you're older, I'll let you read it!

BLOOD FOREVER

My Name Is Sunshine (Sunny) McDonald . . .

. . . and if you'd have asked me a year ago, I would have described myself as a normal, everyday high school sophomore, living a normal, everyday life in normal, everyday suburban Massachusetts. Like many girls my age, I loved English, abhorred math, played varsity field hockey, and auditioned to take part in the school production of *Bye Bye Birdie*. (Mainly to get up close and personal with senior hotness and leading man Jake Wilder, my ultimate normal, everyday crush.)

Back then, just one year ago, I accepted the world exactly how it had been presented to me since birth: normal, logical, and not the least bit supernatural. In fact, if you had asked me to swear on my life that vampires, fairies, werewolves, leprechauns, and other creatures of the night didn't exist (at least outside Stephenie Meyer novels and HBO shows), I'd have happily sworn.

Until that fateful night, that is. The night my dear twin sister, Rayne, dragged me to the oh-so-tacky, Goth haven they call Club Fang—and my sense of normalcy was irreparably shattered forever.

Yes, yes, Sunshine and Rayne. I don't like it any more than you do, so save the jokes. At least the names fit. You see, unlike normal, everyday me, my sister has always embraced the darker side of life. She's basically your typical Goth girl, though she hates being labeled as such. Or labeled at all, I guess. Still, I say, if the Doc Martens fit . . . In any case, she's always been all about dressing in black, listening to morbid music, hanging out in graveyards, wishing she were dead . . .

Or *undead*, as the case may be. Little did I know, while I was busy flirting with Jake and scoring goals, Rayne was occupied getting her vampire certification by taking night school classes at the local coven. She'd been on a waiting list, gotten blood-tested, passed her final exam—she was good to go. And that fateful night at Club Fang I mentioned? That was supposed to be her undead birthday—the day she was meant to be bitten by her vampiric blood mate and become a creature of the night forever.

Ah, romance.

To her, it was a dream come true. Immortality, riches beyond belief, a hot vampire boyfriend, and best of all, no homework. But if you asked me? I'd rather be bogged down with biology any night of the week than sacrifice my tan for all eternity.

Unfortunately, as you may have guessed by now, I didn't get that choice. Due to a bloody bad case of mistaken identity, the vampire in question, Magnus, who was supposed to be Rayne's blood mate, accidentally bit me instead.

Looking back on it now, I can accept the fact that it was an honest mistake. I mean, Rayne and I are so identical even our mother can't tell us apart. So what prayer did Magnus have of discerning our subtle differences? Especially since Rayne made me don that ridiculous BITE ME tank top before heading to the club so I'd better fit in. Which, I guess, worked, if not a little too well.

But though I can accept it now, at the time I was plenty pissed off. Just imagine being told *you're* on your way to being morphed into a vampire—a species that, up until now, you thought was simply a by-product of a dead Victorian author's perverted imagination—one week before prom! So not part of my five-year normal, everyday plan, let me tell you!

But luckily for me it didn't stick. The vampire Magnus was able to make good—figuring out a way to reverse the transformation—and just in time, too. And through our journey together, I ended up realizing he wasn't so bad, under all those fangs. In fact, he was pretty special. And way better than that boring old normal, everyday Jake Wilder of drama club fame.

You gotta understand—while I'm still no fan of bloodsuckers in general, I am a fan of sweet, loyal, protective guys who happen to be former knights in shining armor and now resemble a cross between Ben Barnes and Orlando Bloom. The harder I tried to resist his charms, the more he melted my heart. Today I can't imagine life without him by my side.

In any case, you'd think at this point it'd all slide into some sickeningly sweet happily-ever-after, the end, right? But for us, not so much. You see, Rayne, who still wanted to become a vampire more than anything in the world, suddenly found out from our drama teacher, Mr. Teifert (who, in addition to instructing young thespians, also serves as vice president of an organization called Slayer Inc.), that she was destined to become a vampire slayer. Yes, the girl voted most likely to become a vampire was now officially commissioned to kill them for a living. And she couldn't turn down her destiny either, thanks to a dormant nanovirus the powers-that-be had injected into her bloodstream at birth. Pick another path and *BOOM!* Bye-bye, Rayne.

But don't worry. Slayer Inc. isn't as evil as their name makes them out to be. If anything, they're more like a police force for vampires, voted in more than a hundred years ago to uphold the laws and protect those who followed them, only taking out vamps who broke the rules and became a danger to others. Like Maverick, the first evil vampire Rayne was assigned to slay. He'd planned to take over the coven by creating a deadly virus. My sister, with the help of Blood Coven general Jareth, was able to take him down and save the day. And afterward? She finally got her wish. She became not only a vampire, but Jareth's blood mate for all eternity. (And still a slayer, too! The girl wears many hats, let me tell you.)

We've had a ton of adventures since then. Like when Rayne

had to figure out a way to stop a pack of rampaging werewolf cheerleaders from destroying our hometown. Or when I had to save Magnus from a super sneaky redheaded spy who pretended to be in love with him while spilling coven secrets to her real vampire boyfriend back home. But our biggest adventure of all? Well, it had nothing to do with vampires whatsoever, but rather our parents, who one day broke the news that we weren't normal, everyday humans at all, but rather fairy princesses. Crazy, huh? And let me tell you, Rayne was so not psyched about the glittery pink uniform.

Which brings us to our most current conflict. The one where Magnus and I stopped a fringe group of slayers known as the Alphas from creating an army of vampire-fairy hybrids, using my sister's blood, and letting them loose on the world. A mission impossible that should have made us heroes in the end. But instead we were cast out of the Vampire Consortium for insubordination. Mostly because we had decided that saving vampire kind was more important than playing by power-hungry House Speaker Pyrus's rules.

To make a long story (somewhat) short, we were accused of treason by Pyrus and forced into exile. We hid underneath the streets of New York City, in fear of our lives.

Unfortunately we weren't as safe and sound as we thought we'd be.

Which brings us to where we are today.

Or should I say . . . *when*.

Prologue

"Bertha . . . please . . . don't!"

Rayne's desperate cries echo through the dark, dank tunnels of the New York City underground as the slayer throws her to the ground, scrambling on top of her and digging her nails into my twin's already bleeding flesh. My sister struggles to free herself, but Bertha's got her pinned between muscular thighs, and this time there's no easy escape. I watch in horror, frozen in place, as the slayer rips a wooden stake from its holster and raises it high, ready to bring it down on my sister and steal her away from me forever.

Noooo! I don't even realize I've made the move. But somehow I find myself wrestling Bertha from behind, latching on to her long brown hair and yanking her backward as hard as I can.

"No one stakes my sister, you bitch!" I cry in a voice that

doesn't even sound like mine. I grab her arm and slam it against a nearby cement support beam over and over, until her hand opens and the stake goes clattering to the ground. All I can taste is blood and I realize I must have bitten my own tongue while taking her down.

In the background, I see Rayne struggling to get up, to regain her balance. But she's wounded and woozy and I can tell for a fact she's not ready to jump back into the fray just yet. It's up to me to be the strong one this time. To save my sister as she has always saved me.

Using all my strength, I drag the slayer away, putting distance between her and my twin. If I can only give Rayne enough time to recover, I'm sure she can finish her off. But time is a luxury we don't have. And even with my fairy powers, I don't have the strength to stave off a vampire slayer for long.

Sure enough, with a raging scream, Bertha manages to break free from my grasp, leaving me with nothing more than a handful of nasty hair extensions.

Disgusted, I drop the hair and raise my fists to fight. Bertha grins evilly, my sister forgotten, and makes a deliberate step in my direction. I lunge with all my might, hoping to be able to knock her out somehow. But as I crash into her, she's like solid rock, and a moment later I feel something burning at my forearm. Did she cut me? I can't afford to look down. Instead, I dig my thumbs into her neck as hard as I can, a desperate attempt to cut off her air passageways—something I learned in a self-defense class a long time ago.

My sister joins the fight now, wrestling Bertha away from me. I try to watch, but I'm overcome by dizziness. It's then that I see the knife in the slayer's hand. The one I realize must be made of iron—a deadly substance to fairies. I dare glance down at my arm and see the cut I already guessed was there. A small one, barely visible to the naked eye, but I know, in my heart, it's enough. The poison swims through my veins in dancing blue lines and I find myself falling backward onto the subway rails, just as my sister takes out the slayer once and for all, spilling her blood all over the ground.

"Rayne," I cry, my vision growing spotty. *Oh God. I'm going to die.* I try to reach for my sister, but my arms have become useless and broken. I can vaguely feel Rayne above me, begging me to hold on as she attempts to suck the toxins from my wound. But it's too late. My body convulses as the poison consumes me and a chill seeps through my bones.

"I'm so cold, Rayne," I sob as my sister pulls me into her arms, rocking me close as bloody tears stream down her cheeks. "So . . . cold."

"It's going to be okay," she murmurs. But I know, from the hoarse tone of her voice, that she's lying. It's not going to be okay. This is it. My final moments. When my eyes close, they won't open again. My thoughts flash to Magnus and I wonder, fleetingly, if he survived the fight back at the base with the werewolves, realizing I'll probably never know. The thought hurts worse than the poison.

My beautiful Magnus. My soul mate without a soul. How

can I die without saying good-bye? Without feeling his arms around me one last time. His lips brushing my own, with impossible tenderness. His voice whispering how much he loves me.

But Magnus isn't here. My sister is.

"Rayne," I try to say through chattering teeth. My final words—I need to make them count. I need my sister to know how grateful I am to her, for all she's done for me. For the risks she's taken to keep me safe. I know her all too well—she'll blame herself, decide she's the one responsible for my death, not Bertha. That she could have somehow done more to save me.

But she's wrong. It's not her fault. And it's vital I convince her of this before I take my final breath.

My tongue is thick in my mouth, my brain has gone sluggish, and every word has become the ultimate struggle for release. "You're the best sister a girl could have," I manage to say with great effort. "I . . . love you."

I want to say more—a thousand things more—but the blackness chooses that moment to sweep in and take me away . . . forever.

1

"Sunny! Rayne! Are you two still in bed? The bus will be here in ten minutes!"

I rub my eyes groggily, confused at what sounds like my mother's voice, just outside my bedroom door. Something I know is impossible, since she's off ruling Fairyland and I'm, well, stuck in the land of the dead. The same place I've been hanging out ever since that fateful night under the streets of New York City when Bertha the Vampire Slayer decided to go and kill me.

You know, I have to say, I'm still pretty freaking ticked off about that whole thing, by the way. I mean, hello? She's a vampire slayer. I'm a fairy. Killing me is so not part of her job description. Unfortunately there's really no way to lodge a complaint against her with the powers-that-be from down here in Hades, where I'm stuck for eternity.

I pull the covers over my head and close my eyes, trying to go back to sleep. I'm exhausted after spending most of yesterday playing softball with my dad in the Elysian Fields. I know it sounds bad-daughter-ish to say, but I have to admit, I like the fact that he's dead, too. It's nice to have family around. I only hope when I'm finally judged, they let me stay living with him in his little white picket fence split-level in the nice neighborhood of Elysian Heights instead of sending me off to someplace like Tartarus, where the really evil people go. (Like, imagine trying to borrow a cup of sugar from your neighbors bin Laden and Gaddafi . . .)

"Sunny?" The voice sounds again, this time louder. I reluctantly manage to sit up in bed. It's then that I realize I'm no longer in the cozy little guest bedroom my dad offered to me the day I showed up dead on his doorstep. Instead I somehow appear to be back in my old bedroom in Oakridge, Massachusetts, where we used to live before the fairies came after us and we fled to Vegas. My familiar posters hang on the wall and the patchwork quilt my grandmother made me sits folded at the end of my bed.

Which is completely impossible, of course, seeing as this bedroom, as it looks now, no longer exists. The fairies burned down the entire house months ago.

Which means . . . I sigh, flopping down on my bed . . . I must be having a dream.

A moment later my mother sticks her head through the doorway. She's wearing some kind of long, colorful hemp skirt and peasant blouse, the kind of outfit she used to favor before taking on her current role of Queen of the Light Court. (Fairy wardrobes require a lot more bedazzling.) It makes me smile. What a lovely dream. My old life, nice and normal, just as it used to be long, long ago.

Mom doesn't smile back. Instead, she crosses her arms over her chest, a frown etched on her face. "Sunshine McDonald," she scolds. "Get up this instant. You're going to be late for school."

I contemplate telling her I'm going to skip—after all, dream attendance doesn't affect one's GPA. But then I reconsider. If I manage to stay asleep, all the way to school, I might actually get to dream up some of my old friends and field hockey teammates. That would be pretty awesome—even if they are only figments of my own imagination.

"Sure, Mom," I agree, rolling out of bed, enjoying the feel of soft Victoria's Secret silk pajamas sliding against my skin. Not many people know this, but when you die, you're stuck in the clothing you died in until your judgment day. (Yet another reason it's important to wear clean underwear in case you're in an accident.) The day I died, I'd made an unfortunate wardrobe decision of an itchy wool sweater that I've been regretting ever since.

Mom nods, seemingly satisfied that I'm up for good, then heads out of my room, presumably to go bug my sister. As I search through my closet for a nonitchy outfit, I hear a sudden scream coming from the next room.

What the—? Afraid the dream might be turning nightmare, I rush out of my room and into my sister's. Rayne's got the covers pulled up to her chin and she's staring at Mom as if she's some kind of ghost of Christmas past.

"Oh my God, it worked! It really worked!" she starts babbling, over and over again.

"What worked?" I ask curiously. Her gaze sweeps over to me and she bounds out of bed, throwing her arms around me and squeezing me tight. She's dressed in her favorite Emily the Strange nightgown and I realize she has dirty-blond hair— like she used to before she dyed it last year to differentiate herself from me.

"You're crushing my ribs," I point out. In fact, for a dream hug, it really kind of hurts. I attempt to pry her fingers off me, but she clings on tight, as if she hasn't seen me for years. From the corner of my eye I can see Mom shake her head.

"The bus will be here in less than ten minutes," she announces. "I would like to see you both be on it." And with that, she walks out of the room.

"Ohmigod, ohmigod," Rayne cries, thankfully releasing me from her death hold and bouncing over to her bed. "I can't believe it. It really happened! He really did it!"

"Who did what?" I ask, starting to get a little annoyed. My dream was much more peaceful before Rayne decided to invade it.

My twin turns to me, her eyes wide. "Don't you remember?"

she asks. "Oh, please say you remember. At the very least I need you to know what's going on here. I can't be the only one."

I draw in a slow breath. "Remember what, Rayne?"

Rayne purses her lips, as if she doesn't want to say. Then she pulls me onto the bed and places a hand to my ear. She leans in close. "Hades," she whispers.

I pull away. "Of course I remember Hades, you idiot. I'm stuck there for eternity, after all. Except when I manage to escape for a few blissful dream minutes. Which, I might add, you're not exactly helping me make the most of." I make a move to abandon the bed. But Rayne is too quick—grabbing my hand and jerking me back down.

"Sunny," she says, her voice low and serious. "This is no dream."

Her words send a chill down my spine. "But what else could it be?" I find myself asking, against my better judgment.

She looks at me solemnly. "We've been given another chance."

"Another chance?" I am so lost at this point it's not even funny.

"Look." She draws in a breath. "Remember how I traveled to Hades to free your soul and everything?"

Again with the remember. As if I could forget how, only two days ago, my sister showed up at my dad's front door with her boyfriend, Jareth, and vampire rock star Race Jameson. They had this crazy story about how they planned to make a deal with the devil to get me out. Very sweet of her and all, but, to be honest, I wasn't that optimistic that she could really pull it off. After all, there are only a few people in this world reported to have been brought back from the dead, and most of them are pretty important. Like, Son of God–type important. Why would anyone make an exception for me?

I realize my sister's still talking. "Well, I finally got my audience with Hades, thanks to the help of his wife," she says. "And I begged him to let you out. But he wouldn't. He said it was against the rules or something, and that if he did it for you, he'd have to do it for everyone, yada, yada, yada." Rayne rolls her eyes, telling me exactly what she thinks of that little technicality. "But he owed me—after I helped him win his video game. So we made a bargain anyway."

I bite my lower lip, beginning to get a bad feeling about this. Something about my sister and her so-called bargains, which never seemed to work out in my favor. "Which was . . . ?"

"He reset the clock for us. Basically sent us back in time, into our old bodies. Before any of the badness happened." She dashes to her computer and pulls up the calendar. "See? It's April fifteenth."

I stare at her, realization hitting me with the force of a ten-ton truck. "April fifteenth?" I repeat. "Of last year . . . ?"

"One month and one week before prom," Rayne announces triumphantly. "And . . ."

"One month before Club Fang," I realize aloud. "One month before Magnus bites me by mistake." I stare at my sister, the implications of her so-called bargain hitting me hard and fast. Could it be true? Could we actually be back in time?

"Oh, Rayne," I cry, looking at her with horrified eyes. "What have you done?"

"I've given you a second chance," she says stoutly. "A chance for you to choose your destiny once and for all." She pauses, then adds, "Are you willing to take it?"

2

Back in time. My stomach flip-flops as I stare at my sister, trying to make sense of it all. Back in time?

Rayne's done some crazy stuff before, don't get me wrong, but nothing like this. My mind races as I try to catalog the events of the past year. All the life-changing stuff we've experienced. All the supernatural events. Vampires, werewolves, fairies. Everything that happened to us . . . has it really now unhappened?

Rayne's hopeful smile fades, her enthusiasm sliding into nervousness as she waits for me to say something . . . anything. I shake my head, not knowing whether I should kiss her or kill her. I mean, she did manage to do the impossible—to bring me back to life. But at what cost?

"I'm sorry, Sun," my sister says after a time, her voice thick with regret. "I know it's a lot to take in. And believe me, I didn't make the decision lightly. But Hades left me no choice. He's really a 'my way or the highway' type of guy, if you want to know the truth. And not half as good at video games as he thinks he is."

I lie back on the bed, staring up at the ceiling. Long ago, when we were kids, Rayne and I had pasted glow-in-the-dark stars up there and some of them had stayed stuck. Unlike my reality, that is, which has suddenly become completely unglued.

"Magnus," I whisper, finally admitting aloud what's been niggling at the back of my mind. My sweet vampire. What happened to him when time reset? Did he lose all memory of me and the things we'd shared over the last year? Does the Magnus in this time period even know I exist?

I let out an involuntary gasp at the thought. All those moments, all those memories, stolen away. Rayne lies down beside me, also staring up at the ceiling. "Yeah," she says. "That's the worst part. I had to leave Jareth behind, too."

I turn to glance at her, pulled out of my self-pity for a moment as it hits me exactly what my sister's given up for me. She could have easily left me to rot in the Underworld and gone off to live happily ever after with her vampire boyfriend. But now, just like Magnus, Jareth won't know her from a hole in the wall. She's given up her true love—her eternal happiness—all for my second chance.

"I'm sorry, Rayne," I whisper, reaching over to squeeze her hand.

"I can't tell you what it was like," she says, choking on her words. "To have to sit there and tell him I'm leaving him, only moments after promising I'd stay by his side forever." Her voice cracks on the word *forever* and I realize she's lost something else in addition to her love. She's no longer a vampire. No longer immortal. Everything she's ever wanted in life has been ripped away. For me.

"Why did you do it?" I ask. "I mean, you could have just left me there . . ." Her sacrifice is so stunning, it's hard for me to come to terms with it.

"Because I knew in my heart it was for the best," she says simply. "It wasn't just your death. Everything was bad. Magnus had been caught by Pyrus's wolves and would be tried for treason. The vampires in the Blood Coven had been kicked out of the Consortium and would have had to live a life of starvation and exile." She turns her head to look at me, her eyes pleading for my understanding. "I couldn't bear to let everyone suffer because of my mistakes."

"Rayne, it wasn't your fault—"

But she waves me off. "That's not important now. What's important is you have a second chance," she insists. "A chance to live the life you were supposed to live. A normal life without vampires and other supernatural surprises. Without all the darkness I dragged you into that night when Magnus bit you instead of me."

My mind flashes back to that fateful night at Club Fang. The moment my life changed forever. Would I have done things differently if I knew then what I know now?

I guess I'll find out soon enough.

3

"Hey, Sunny, you ready for the big game tonight?"

I turn around as my old friend and field hockey team-mate Amanda taps me on the shoulder in the lunch line at school that afternoon. Wow. I haven't seen her since—

Yesterday. Sunny, you haven't seen her since yesterday. At least in her mind.

"Oh, totally," I force myself to say, trying to keep my voice as casual as possible. It's been so weird seeing all these people I haven't seen since Rayne and I left Oakridge High for Vegas last November. Especially since to them, no time has passed at all. "As ready as I'll ever be."

"Good," Amanda pronounces, looking relieved. "When you weren't in homeroom first period, I got worried. We have *got* to win this match against Haverhill tonight or we are totally screwed for the rest of the season."

"I know, right?" I find myself saying, trying hard to muster up an appropriate level of concern over some random high school sporting event that I couldn't care less about. I mean, really. Winning? Losing? What did it matter in the long run? It wasn't as if anyone's life were at stake. As if an evil vampire would take over the town and cause mass destruction if we didn't score a goal. Heck, I played the same game the first time around and I can't even remember what the outcome was.

It's funny. I thought I'd be so psyched to get back to school. To go back to my former life and see all my old friends. But so far the first day back had been nothing short of a total nightmare. And not one of those dramatic, freaky nightmares that at least would be interesting. It was more like that movie *Groundhog Day*, where I felt as if I'd already lived it a thousand times before.

"By the way, I heard Jake Wilder might be stopping by the game tonight," Amanda adds, giving me a not-so-subtle wink.

Jake Wilder. Wow. I'd almost forgotten he even existed. It's hard to believe the resident school Sex God—the one I crushed on hardcore back in the day—was once a very important person in my life. Thinking back, I can't even remember what I saw in him. I guess he was good looking. And popular. But he couldn't hold a candle to Magnus. The most wonderful boyfriend in the entire universe.

Who I'd probably never see again.

Before heading to school, Rayne and I had made a pact. To

live a normal, vampire-free life from this point forward. Too much badness had happened, my sister reasoned, because of our dalliances in the otherworld. It was better for all involved if we stayed out of it altogether and lived normal, everyday lives from this point forward.

But though in my head I knew she was right, my heart was singing a different song. How could I ever waste time going after someone like Jake Wilder, when I knew someone like Magnus existed on the fringes of my reality?

I get my lunch—some nasty, dried-up chicken nuggets and fries—and follow Amanda over to the table where the rest of my team appears to be debating the various pros and cons of different brands of lip gloss with quite a bit of venom, considering the subject matter.

"Oh-Em-Gee, are you for real?" Olivia cries in disgust. "That stuff is like liquid glue! The one time I wore it, I almost got stuck to Carter permanently when I kissed him!"

"As if that's a bad thing," Ava shot back with a devious smile on her lips.

"Please," cut in Jessica. "I make my own lip gloss. All you need is a little beeswax. A little honey . . ."

"So, um, anyone hear about that crazy terrorist attack over in Syria this weekend?" I butt in, after checking my phone for a time-appropriate current event. "Pretty scary, right?"

The girls turn to look at me as if I have three heads and have just announced that I enjoy waterboarding over the weekends for fun.

"Um, yeah. Scary," Olivia says quickly. Then she turns back

to Jessica. "So wait. You make your own? But can you tint it that way? I much prefer tinted gloss . . ."

Oh God. I rise from my seat and flee the inane conversation, purposely leaving my inedible lunch behind me. Was this really what my friends thought was important? Had I once thought it was important, too? Then I remember the ridiculous amount of lip gloss I'd pawed through this morning in my bathroom drawer trying to find a tube of toothpaste. Evidently so.

But not anymore. Try as I might, I can't seem to bring myself to care about lip gloss or field hockey games or cute boys with no personalities. I can't care about English or math or getting good grades. All these things that once took priority in my so-called normal life now seem flat and dull and ridiculous.

I have to face it: I'm not that girl anymore. That innocent, naive creature who flitted through life without a care in the world for anything but her own well-being. And I can't go back to being her, no matter how hard I try. Not when I know what's out there, under the surface of our world. The battles, the chaos, the intrigue. And most important, the most beautiful, sweet, loving vampire in the entire universe.

The one who no longer knows I exist.

I scan the cafeteria, catching sight of my sister, sitting and laughing with her best friend, Spider, as if no time at all has passed between them. My hackles rise. How can she be adjusting so nicely when I'm feeling like I'm in the freaking Twilight Zone? I stomp over in her direction.

"But Rayne, there's no such thing as a level eighty mage!" I hear Spider protest as I approach. "And I've never heard of that spell . . ."

"Oh. Right." Rayne looks suddenly flustered as she sees me approach. "Well, I think it's . . . um, in the next expansion pack?" She looks up at me and smiles nervously. "Hey, Sunny!" she cries. "How's it going?"

"I don't see anything listed here about a new expansion pack," Spider mutters, staring down at her phone while my sister shoots me a *Save me!* look.

"Rayne, I've got to talk to you," I butt in, now realizing that perhaps my sister isn't fitting in quite as well as it first appeared. I shouldn't be happy about that, but I kind of am. "Alone."

"Sorry, Spider," Rayne says quickly, a look of relief washing over her face. "Can I catch you later?" She leaps up from her seat and follows me to an empty table. Once we're seated, she wipes her brow. "Thank God," she says. "I had no idea how hard it was to remember which game updates happened when." She presses a few buttons on her phone. "I could have sworn the two-point-three patch had come out by now . . ."

I roll my eyes. "Um, can you review your game history on your own time?"

"Oh. Sorry." She looks up, stuffing her phone in her pocket. "What's going on? Are you having fun in your old life? Did you get to see some of your friends? Have you found Jake Wilder yet? Is he as hot as you remember him? Maybe you should ask him to prom. I mean, since this time around you don't have that magical vampire scent to attract him and get him to ask you—"

"Rayne," I interrupt. "I can't take it anymore. It's all too vapid and boring. I mean, no one here cares about anything but dressing up and hooking up—and not necessarily in that order."

"Well, evidently a few people are interested in the nuances of game patch releases . . ."

"Rayne! I'm serious," I cry, giving her a pleading look. "What's wrong with me? I should be overjoyed to spend long hours discussing the benefits and drawbacks of various lip glosses."

My sister raises a skeptical eyebrow.

"Don't mock! I used to love that kind of thing," I confess. "And yet now all I want to do is take a tube of it and shove it up my best friend's nose—to get her to stop talking!"

"You've come a long way, young grasshopper."

"I used to love high school." I sigh. "Everything about it. Even the homework wasn't so bad. But now, just sitting in my classes, knowing I'm wasting my life away . . ." I look up sadly. "I can't take it."

My sister laughs bitterly. "*You* can't!" she exclaims. "What about me? I didn't like it the first time around. That's half the reason I went and got my vampire certification to begin with. To get the hell out of this place." My twin shakes her head. "By all rights, I should be going to my vampire-in-training class tonight, getting ready for my undead transformation. Not stuck arguing video game semantics with a fire mage who evidently has the entire Vampires vs. Zombies wiki memorized."

I look at her thoughtfully. I'd forgotten all about that little three-month training class she took to first qualify to become a vampire. I guess that would be going on right about now, one month before her graduation.

"And you're not going to go this time?" I ask curiously.

Rayne shrugs. "What would be the point? It'd only start the badness all over again. And we'd end up right back where we started. Let's face it, our best bet is to forget the whole vampire thing altogether and learn to live as mortals in this brave new world."

"Boring new world, more like," I say with a moan.

"*Normal* new world," Rayne counters. "The kind of world you said you always wanted to live in, I might add. A world with no crazy, death-defying adventures. No super-secret conspiracies. A world where Mom lives at home and Dad isn't dead. And neither are you. I mean, you have to admit, being stuck in algebra class is still better than being stuck in Hades. At least you have a chance to pass algebra and move on."

"A very slight chance," I snort. Half of me wants to say high school is worse than the seventh circle of Hell, but then I catch the hopeful look on her face and force myself to nod in agreement instead. After all, she could have just left me there and gone on with her own life. But no, she did all this for me. At the very least, I need to act grateful.

"It's not that I don't appreciate being here," I assure her. "I just . . . well, I miss Magnus. It's so crazy to know that he's out there, somewhere, and I have no idea where."

"Well, that's not entirely true," Rayne clarifies. "I mean, we know where he'll be tonight, obviously."

My heart skips a beat. "We do?"

"Well, yeah. He'll be at the vampire-in-training class. Actually, this was the first night the two of us ever met," Rayne explains. "But don't worry, like I said, I won't be going this time around," she adds. "I'm totally committed to staying vampire free from this point forward as promised. No matter what."

"Me, too," I find myself echoing. "Vampire free, that's me."

But my mind has other ideas . . .

4

I resist the nearly irresistible urge to reach up under my black-and-red-trimmed corset to give my bellybutton a good solid scratch. Seriously, I don't know how the heck Rayne wears this Goth stuff every day of the week. It is so majorly uncomfortable, what with the thick black lace rubbing my armpits raw and the corset bones digging into my waist, making it nearly impossible to take in a full breath. And that's not even mentioning the smoosh factor going on with my already admittedly small breasts. Seriously, give me a pair of Old Navy boot-cut jeans, tank top, and flip-flops any day of the week, thank you very much. Sure, they may not qualify me to rock a runway, but at least I'm able to take advantage of my full lung capacity.

But unfortunately tonight my own "uniform" just won't cut it. Not if I want to fool the vampires down at Blood Coven

University into thinking I'm my twin sister, that is. Rayne wouldn't be caught dead in jeans, which means that I must suffer through the agony and humiliation of sneaking out of the house in full-on Goth gear, complete with fluffy tulle skirt, ripped fishnets, and black boots with six-inch platform soles, all dug out of her jam-packed black-on-black-on-black closet.

I know, I know. I shouldn't be doing this. And Rayne would freaking kill me if she found out I was. (Even before she learned it was in her clothes.) After all, the whole point behind this life "do-over" my sister arranged with the Lord of the Underworld was designed to give us the opportunity to go back to living a normal, vampire-free life. And if Rayne—the girl who loves vampires more than anything in the universe—is able to simply walk away from her vampire-in-training class, what the heck am I doing, choosing to attend in her stead?

But let's be honest here; what would *you* do if you had the opportunity to catch a glimpse of your true love one last time? Could you just walk away—go see a movie instead? Yeah, I didn't think so. And hey, it's not like I'm going to go make out with the guy and declare my eternal devotion or anything. I'm just going to gaze upon him, quietly, from across the room. Take one last, longing look before I go back to my pathetic, normal, Magnus-free life, forever.

Besides, it's not like I could do any more than that, even if I wanted to. This Magnus, the one who exists in this time period, doesn't think of me as his girlfriend. He's not in love with me. He doesn't want to be with me. And, if we do happen to cross paths, he's just going to assume I'm my sister. So no big deal.

Except, of course, it kind of is. It's kind of the biggest deal ever.

No. I shake my head. *I won't go there.* What we're doing is for the best. Like my sister said, if I never befriend Magnus, we'll never end up together. He'll never have to make the choice between the Blood Coven and me, and thus none of the badness that has happened over the last year will happen. I won't die. He won't be tried for treason. And the Blood Coven won't be kicked out of the Consortium. Everyone will live happily ever after.

And I'm totally down for all that to happen. After I get my one last look.

The vampire-in-training class is being held right outside Saint Patrick's Cemetery—the secret location of Blood Coven HQ, not that I'm supposed to know that. The location of the vampire crypt is strictly classified until you become a full-blooded member. So instead they hold classes in a nearby former church, which seems a totally weird option, until you learn that this particular church has been long ago de-holyized and put out of official commission. Meaning the ground is no longer hallowed and perfectly fine and safe for vampire feet to walk over.

I head up the wooden front steps and through the front door, resisting the urge to roll my eyes at some of Rayne's fellow vampire-in-training classmates who are standing outside smoking. I mean, hello? Could you be any more stereotypical if you tried? Every single one of them is dolled up in their Gothy best, complete with black (and/or hot-pink) hair, pancake-white makeup, and an inordinate amount of piercings. Seriously, doesn't anyone outside the Goth scene want to become a vampire anymore? I mean, you'd think with the whole *Twilight* phenomenon we'd get a few Bellas out here at the very least.

"Name, please?"

I glance down at the bored-looking receptionist sitting at a card table just inside the front door. My eyes widen as I realize it's none other than Marcia herself, Magnus's former secretary. Of course right now, I guess, she's his future secretary, still working for Lucifent, who's currently Master of the Blood Coven. It's not till Bertha slays Lucifent and Magnus takes over that she starts working for her new boss. (This time-travel stuff can be very confusing even if you are paying attention.)

"Um, are you deaf?" Marcia demands, her face twisting into a scowl. "I said, what is your name?"

Yup. She's exactly the same. I bite back a frown, pinning my arms to my sides so as to avoid reaching my hands out and involuntarily strangling that haughty look right off her face. Bitch. After all, it's because of her that Pyrus learned of our secret location under the streets of New York City. Because of her that I'm dead in the future. But what can I do? Accuse her of a crime she's yet to commit? That'll be sure to go off well. And besides, seeing as she's a vampire and I'm just a puny mortal, I admit I might have a tough time cutting off her air supply using nothing more than my bare hands.

Gotta live and let live, I suppose. At least for now.

"S—I mean Rayne McDonald," I reply instead, trying my best to sound as bored as she. She scans her list and checks me off, snapping her gum in an apparent effort to let me know how insignificant I am to her existence. If only she knew.

"You can go over and sit there," she informs me, pointing a perfectly manicured finger to the left side of the church, where another group of Goths have congregated. Across the aisle, I notice a much more mainstream crowd hanging out chatting. The vampires themselves, I realize. Unlike their trying-too-hard mortal trainees, the vampires are dressed casually. Jeans, T-shirts, sundresses . . . and . . . I do a double take . . . is that really the same pink BITE ME tank top I ended up wearing on that fateful trip to Club Fang? The one that started all the trouble in the first place? I remember Rayne telling me she borrowed it off some vampire she met in training . . .

As I make my way over to the mortal section, I suddenly catch a glimpse of a door at the front of the church swinging open. I stop in my tracks, my heart skipping a beat, as a lone vampire steps out into the sanctuary.

Magnus.

My world spins off its axis as I watch him stop and stand just behind the altar, scanning the room with disinterested eyes. He looks bored, a little annoyed, and totally and utterly hot. My mind treats me to a vivid flashback of that first night we met at Club Fang. He was dressed in simple but elegant Armani, just like today, and I remember thinking he looked exactly like Orlando Bloom from the first *Pirates* movie, with his shoulder-length chestnut-colored hair tied back with a simple leather strap.

Tonight his hair hangs free, falling into his elfish blue eyes, brushing against his perfectly sculptured cheekbones and ending just short of his sensuous mouth. Suddenly I find myself with the inability to think of anything else in the world except for him, taking me into his arms and pressing those full, soft lips against my own, with a reverence and worship I've never fully deserved.

Oh, Magnus . . . I find myself stepping forward, my heart aching in my chest. *Oh, my love* . . .

He turns, raking a hand through his hair and clearing it from his face. His gaze locks onto mine, his eyes zeroing in on my own. I swallow hard and find myself giving him a small, hopeful wave and smile. But instead of smiling back—instead of his eyes lighting up as they fall upon my face—he merely raises a perfectly arched eyebrow, his beautiful lips curling into a small sneer as he gives me a critical once-over before turning away.

My heart plummets as reality comes crashing back down on me. He doesn't know me. He doesn't love me. All he can see is some stupid overdressed vampire wannabe stranger, just like the rest, making googly eyes at him from across the room. Ugh. What possessed me to dress like my sister tonight? I've only succeeded in repulsing my own boyfriend with a tacky outfit that isn't even me.

Which is a good thing, I try to remind myself. The last thing I want is for him to be attracted to me when I'm supposed to stay far, far away.

But still, it hurts. Especially as I watch him walk over to one of the other vampires—the girl in the BITE ME tank—and whisper something in her ear. She turns and looks over in my direction, chuckling. Are they really making fun of me? My face burns in a mixture of embarrassment and fury.

What am I doing? Why am I even here? I should have stayed away—then I could have lived out the rest of my life, only remembering Magnus gazing upon me with adoration and love. Now I'll be forced to remember his look of scorn and derision until my dying day.

I stumble toward the exit, my vision blurring with tears. I need to get out of here and fast. Before I dissolve in a pathetic puddle of lovelorn goo.

Unfortunately my escape attempt does not go as smoothly as I planned—mostly because I'm just not used to running around in boots with six-inch soles. So instead of slipping out the door and vanishing into the night, I find myself stumbling head over heels, crashing into a standing candelabra before becoming one with the marble floor.

The room, predictably, erupts in laughter. And here I thought my face couldn't get any redder.

"Are you okay?"

I look up toward the sound of a familiar female voice. My eyes widen as I find none other than Charity herself—one of Magnus's blood donors—looming above me, a worried look on her face. Without waiting for me to answer, she helps me up and leads me over to a nearby pew. I can feel the amused stares of all the vampires and mortals as I collapse onto the bench, but I force myself to ignore them.

"Thanks," I say, letting out a long breath. "Sorry, just lost my footing there for a moment."

She plops down beside me and reaches into her bag, pulling out a large chocolate chip cookie. "Eat this," she instructs. "I find a little sugar helps when you're all weak in the knees."

I take the cookie gratefully. After all, she should know about weak knees, being a blood donor and all. She's probably used to living life a pint or two short. And I appreciate her kindness—it's more than I can say about anyone else in the room. "Thanks," I say, taking a bite of the cookie. "I appreciate it."

"I'm Charity," she says, holding out a hand. "I assume you're one of the trainees?"

I nod. "I'm Sun—I mean, Rayne McDonald," I say, shaking her hand.

Her eyes widen with interest. "Rayne McDonald?" she repeats. "So you're—"

A shadow looms above us, cutting off her question. "There you are, Charity. You're wanted in the back. Rachel tells me it's time for your draining."

Oh God. My throat goes dry. I'd know that deep, English-accented voice anywhere. If it were a thousand years since I'd heard it, I'd still know it better than my own. My hands start shaking uncontrollably and I quickly shove them under my thighs.

Don't look up. Whatever you do, don't look up. Keep your eyes glued to the floor until he walks away and out of your life forever.

But, of course, there's no way I can do that.

And so I find myself gazing upon his beautiful face, my eyes falling helplessly into his own sapphire ones, framed by thick, black lashes. *This is just Magnus,* I try to scold my quickly melting heart. *You've spent hours and days locked in his embrace. It should be no big deal to look at him.*

But it is. It's like the biggest deal ever.

"Very well, Master," Charity says, rising to her feet and lowering her gaze in deference to the vampire. "I will go to Rachel right away. I know you must get very hungry on a night like tonight."

Her words startle me out of my trance. "Night like tonight?" I find myself blurting out, realizing I have no idea what people actually do here at vampire training school. What could Magnus be up to that would require an extra pint of blood?

Magnus gives me a hard look. "Bite night," he replies stiffly, as if it's a burden to even lower himself to speak to me. He starts turning back to Charity.

"Magnus," the blood donor hisses in a distinct stage whisper. "This is Rayne McDonald. Your, well . . ." She pauses, biting her lower lip, looking from her master to me. "You know . . ."

"Your future blood mate," I finish, rising to my feet and giving him an awkward smile. "At your service."

Magnus's face goes stark white. He looks at Charity, then at me, then back at his blood donor. I know exactly what he's thinking. *You're telling me I'm going to be stuck with this tacky fashion victim for all of eternity?* If it weren't so tragic, it'd almost be comical.

The silence that follows is suffocating. My heart feels as if it's been squeezed in a vise. "Maybe I should go," I stammer. "This was a bad idea." *On so many levels.*

I turn away so he won't see the tears spring to my eyes. I should leave. I should bolt out of this old, decommissioned church and never look back. But as I take that first step, I feel a strong hand on my arm. I turn back to see Magnus's sheepish face.

"Wait," he says, his voice filled with guilt. He always was a softie—underneath that tough exterior. "I'm sorry. I think we've gotten off on the wrong foot. Please forgive me." He releases my arm and bows his head reverently. "It is lovely to meet you, Rayne McDonald," he says. Almost as if he actually means it.

"Yeah," I manage to reply, though it's quite an effort getting any words past the lump in my throat. He must think I'm a total freak. "Um, great to meet you, too." Out of habit, I stick out my hand. I can't believe I'm actually giving my soul mate a friendly handshake. What the hell was I thinking coming here in the first place? This is torture worse than any fiery circle of Hell.

In response, he slips his hand into my own, squeezing it with tempered vampire strength. My whole body explodes at his touch, and it's all I can do not to cry out loud.

Oh, Magnus. My love . . .

He drops my hand like a hot potato and my first reaction is to be offended all over again. But then I catch the shadow crossing his face, the glimmer of confusion in his eyes. Ha! He feels it, too. Despite his best efforts, he feels something of the magnetic attraction between us. Just that simple fact makes me feel a little better.

I watch, breath in my throat, as he swallows hard, then turns to Charity, who's watching the scene with apparent amusement. "Why the hell are you still here?" he demands angrily, taking out his confusion on the only target he can.

"I'm not! I'm gone!" she assures him, dancing down the aisle and toward the back door, leaving me alone with Magnus again. My heart pounds in my chest as I search for something intelligent to say.

"So, um, Bite Night?" I try. "What's that?" It's all I can come up with on short notice with my body still humming from his touch.

He shakes his head before replying, as if trying to regain some semblance of control over his traitorous body. "Well," he says, "as you know, in one month, when you complete your vampire training, the two of us will share one another's blood, bonding as blood mates . . . for eternity."

"Right," I reply, nodding. "I know that part." Of course, unbeknownst to him, by then I'll be far, far away. Forgetting he even exists for the good of all humanity and vampire kind. I wonder what he'll think when he finds out I bailed. Will he be disappointed? Relieved?

"Well," he continues, clearing his throat. "On Bite Night we practice."

"Um, what?" My pulse picks up all over again as I give him a questioning look. "Practice what?"

His cheeks pinken into a blush, and for a moment I think he's not going to explain. But then he shrugs and looks up, piercing me with his hot blue eyes and melting me all over again.

"Why, biting you, of course."

5

stare at Magnus in shock, one hundred percent positive, even without looking into a mirror, that my face has drained of all its color. (Which, unfortunately, probably only serves to make me look even more like a Goth girl. Yuck.)

"Did you say . . . bite me? As in biting me on the neck? Biting me on the neck with your fangs?" I stammer nonsensically, seeming unable to utter anything even remotely intelligent. After all, what else could he mean? It's not like the phrase *Why, biting you, of course* is all that ambiguous to begin with.

But still! What am I going to do? I mean, sure, it's one thing to show up and stare at Magnus from across the room one last time. Quite another to agree to having his lips press against my neck, his fangs slicing through my flesh. Not that I'm worried about physical injury or anything—I know I'll heal. It's just that

I also know all too well from previous experience how heavenly it can feel for a vampire—any vampire—to bite a mortal on the neck. And this isn't just any vampire. This is Magnus. My Magnus.

I so cannot do this.

"Are you okay?" Magnus asks, peering at me with concern. "You look as if you're about to pass out."

"I'm fine," I blurt out quickly. "It's only that . . . I guess I didn't realize that we were doing the whole biting thing tonight. And well, I'm feeling a little under the weather, actually." I fake a sneeze, then cough loudly into my hand for effect. "You might not want to bite me tonight. I mean, you wouldn't want to catch my cold. Or flu . . . Yeah, actually, now that I think about it, I might have the flu. Or maybe that nasty superbug that's going around?" I suggest hopefully. "In fact, just the other day I heard someone say something about a global pandemic that the government is trying to cover up. I wouldn't want you catching it and ending up turning into a zombie or something, all on my account . . ." I trail off, looking at him helplessly. He isn't buying any of this. I can tell. Not that I blame him.

Sure enough, Magnus raises a skeptical eyebrow. "I'm an immortal, all-powerful creature of the night," he reminds me drolly. "I don't catch colds."

Oh. Right. Duh. I'm an idiot. Of course he can't get sick. I should have remembered that from the one time I really did come down with the flu and he stayed by my bedside feeding me chicken soup until dawn. Which was so very sweet of him, I might add.

I shake my head. No. I have to think of some other excuse. Something else to get me out of the whole biting thing. Not that half of me doesn't want him to go for it. I mean, to be honest, I really can't think of anything better than having my true love's lips against my neck. (Well, besides having them against my lips, that is.) But I know all too well that if I allow that to happen, I'll be a goner for sure. And there'll be no way I'll be able to walk out of his life forever.

Which I really need to do. Not only for myself. But for him. And Jareth. And the rest of the Blood Coven. Their entire future depends on me not screwing this up.

Magnus puts a hand on my shoulder. "Look, it probably seems scarier than it is," he says. "But trust me, it's not a big deal. I won't even be drawing any blood. And I'll put numbing cream on my fangs beforehand. You won't feel a thing."

"I know, I know," I say. God, he must think I'm a total baby. "It's just . . . It's just . . ." What am I supposed to say? *It's just that I'm back from the future and don't want to fall in love with you all over again?*

Magnus's face softens. He gestures for me to take my seat again, then sits down beside me. "Look," he says, peering into my eyes with his own deep-blue ones. "If you're feeling uncomfortable, we don't need to do this tonight. You can go home and spend some time thinking things through."

I cock my head in question. "Thinking things through?" What is he talking about?

He gives me a rueful look. "Look, Rayne. If you can't even bring yourself to go through with a practice bite, do you really think you're ready for the real thing?" he asks slowly. "Because if you're not, I suggest you walk away now, while you still have a chance at mortality. Remember, eternal life is forever. And forever is a long time to live with regret."

I drop my eyes, conflicting thoughts waging war inside my head. Poor Magnus. I know how much he wants a blood mate. He's been so lonely. By himself for a millennium. This is his one chance to find a partner in crime to spend eternity with, and I know how much he's been looking forward to it. And yet he's willing to let me go. To remain alone so I won't have to do something I might regret. It's so sweet and selfless I can hardly stand it.

And I find I can't bring myself to let him down. At least not today.

"I'm okay," I assure him, daring to rest a hand on his arm. It's all I can do not to yank him toward me and wrap him into a huge hug. But that would be seriously improper, I know. Not to mention more than a bit awkward, seeing as we're supposed to have just met mere minutes before. "I know what I'm doing."

Yeah, I know what I'm doing all right. Risking the future of the world, as well as my own life, in order to avoid disappointing a single vampire. A single vampire, I might add, who would not exactly appreciate the gesture, if he knew what I was doing. Magnus has always been perfectly clear about the idea that his own happiness comes second to that of the Blood Coven vampires under his care. I remember him freaking out at Jareth under the streets of New York City, moments before my death, because Jareth chose to try to save him—out of love and friendship—and inadvertently endangered his people.

But they're not his people now, I realize. At this point in time, the former Blood Coven Master, Lucifent, is still alive. And Magnus is simply another member of the coven, with no responsibility to anyone but himself. I sigh. If only he could stay that way. If only Slayer Inc. didn't have to go and slay Lucifent and force Magnus to take over in his stead.

Oh my God, that's it! My mind races with the possibility. If we could prevent Lucifent's murder somehow, then Magnus wouldn't become Master. And if Magnus doesn't become Master, he won't run the risk of pissing off Pyrus. And if he doesn't piss off Pyrus, then the Blood Coven won't be kicked out of the Consortium. Magnus won't be tried for treason and Bertha will have no reason to kill me.

Everyone will live happily ever after. And Magnus will be free to be my boyfriend forever.

My heart pounds with excitement as a plan forms in my mind. Could something like this really work? I mean, I know we're talking about dangerous history-changing stuff here, which, let's face it, didn't work out all that well in any of the *Back to the Future* movies. But in this case, the future is going to change regardless, right? So what would be the big deal about tweaking it a little bit more to ensure the absolute best outcome?

What if Lucifent didn't have to die? I mean, the reason for his death was pretty ridiculous to begin with. Who goes and murders someone just because he's trapped in a body of a child? Slayer Inc. says child vampires are an abomination. But Magnus always told me Lucifent was a good leader and didn't deserve what came his way. If we could stop his death, we could make everything right!

My excited thoughts are interrupted as a tall, thin vampire, dressed in a Fangtasia T-shirt, walks up the pulpit and bangs his gavel. A hush falls over the crowd as humans and vampires look up expectantly. "It is time," he announces in a gravelly voice. He reaches for a remote control and holds it up to a projector screen. The words *Biting 101* appear, soundtracked by some pretty cheesy elevator music.

"There's an instructional video?" I ask incredulously, forgetting my plan for a moment. "Really? I mean, can't you just point and chomp?" After all, it looks pretty easy in the movies . . .

Magnus chuckles. "Sure. But point and chomp on the wrong vein and your blood mate won't live long enough to earn her fangs."

Yikes. "Well, I guess we should practice then," I say resignedly. "Lots and lots of practice." Great. As if having his lips touch my neck once isn't already one time too many.

The video cuts to a blond vampire, dressed in black and sitting in a cushy armchair. My eyes widen as I realize who it is. None other than Pyrus himself. The Consortium House Speaker. The man who, in the future, will issue our death warrants. A shiver trips down my spine and it's all I can do not to drop down and try to hide under a pew. I have to remind myself that one, this is a prerecorded video and he's actually not in the room, and two, even if he were, he doesn't have a crystal ball to see into the future. To him, I'm simply another *Twilight*-loving vamp wannabe, of no significance to his unlife whatsoever.

But still. Super-creepy to see him on the big screen. Especially since no one in the room besides me knows what he's capable of. Or *will* be capable of, that is. "Good evening, vampires," he says in a deep, throaty voice. "And congratulations on reaching the one-thousand-year mark."

The room erupts in applause as mortals clap for their future blood mates. Wow, I'd totally forgotten about that part. A vampire literally has to live a thousand years before they let him or her have a partner in crime. Which is a long time not to date, if you ask me.

"It's quite an accomplishment," Pyrus continues. "And we're looking forward to spending the next thousand years with you and your blood mates in our service." I scowl. Yeah, servicing Pyrus and his dictatorship. If only these people knew what they were really signing up for when they cast their lot with this jerk.

"And welcome to our new recruits as well," Pyrus purrs, his eyes seeming to rove the audience. "You are the best of the best. Hand chosen by our experts for your superior DNA and high-level IQ. I am certain each and every one of you will make fine additions to your new covens, and become loyal servants to the Worldwide Vampire Consortium for all eternity."

A spattering of applause ripples through the crowd. Eager mortals who have no idea what they're actually clapping for cheer for the man on the screen. As I sit there, listening to Pyrus drone on about responsibility and dedication, a feeling of dread and realization starts creeping into my bones.

Right now I'm the only one on earth who knows what this vampire is capable of. What will happen if his reign is allowed to continue unchecked. Well, my sister and I, that is. We're the only ones who know how much damage he can cause if allowed to stay in power.

So even putting aside the whole selfish I-want-Magnus-as-my-boyfriend-again thing, how can we rightly sit back and go on living normal lives, forgetting vampires exist, when Pyrus is still in charge? Sure, if we stay out of it, he won't be coming after us. Or maybe not even the Blood Coven. But judging from his track record, he's bound to hurt someone else instead.

We can't let him do that.

Pyrus says something randomly inspirational, everyone claps again, and the video fades to black. The doors open up and blood donors start wheeling out plastic torsos to each vampire, like it's a CPR class or something. I guess you practice on dummies before you start on the real dummies. The ones who think becoming one of Pyrus's people is actually a good idea.

But I have no time to play these reindeer games. I have to find my sister. I rise from the pew, turning to Magnus with a regretful smile. "I'm sorry," I say. "Can we take a rain check on the bite? There's something I have to do."

6

Rayne

I should probably stay home and play video games tonight. After all, I no longer have my vampire-certification class to go to. And Sunny's not home, probably off celebrating her team's field hockey victory or something. So it stands to reason that I should stay home and load up my computer, right? Maybe offer up some futuristic video game leetness to my fellow players of the past? I can just imagine their faces when I totally rock that World of Warcraft dungeon no one in this time period has been able to master yet. And maybe I'd even score that amazing one-handed fire sword that the last boss ends up dropping sometimes.

Or I could always hang out with Mom, I suppose. Spend some quality time with her and take advantage of the fact that she's lazing around on our couch in flannel pajamas instead of off in another dimension, playing high queen to the Fairyland Light Court. It might be nice, actually, to curl up with her under the afghan, diving into a carton of dairy-free ice cream with an extra large spoon and watching the latest episodes of our favorite TV shows.

I should do either of those things. Or, you know, something else completely normal and ordinary and vampire free. I made a promise to Sunny, after all. And besides, what good is a second chance if you start doing the same things you did the first time around?

But try as I might, I can't seem to bring myself to turn on the computer and search for a party. Or plop down on the couch and content myself with television. Maybe it's because I know that the so-called amazing one-handed fire sword I might score will be practically worthless in a few months after the powers-that-be update the game. Or because while spending time with Mom is always nice, everything on TV is bound to be a repeat for me.

So instead, against my better judgment, I find myself opening up my closet and rummaging through, selecting a red-and-black Goth Loli dress with matching red cape and black platform boots. After donning the outfit, I head into the bathroom to make up my face with my favorite white powder, kohl eyeliner, and bloodred lipstick. Gothing it up to go out.

I have to say, it's so weird looking at my reflection in the mirror and seeing a blond girl staring back at me. I look so much like Sunny, even with the makeup on—no wonder Magnus wasn't able to tell us apart on that fateful night. I vow to swing by the twenty-four-hour drugstore on the way home and buy a bottle of black dye. Mom will kill me all over again for doing it, but it's a punishment worth undergoing twice if only to stand out again.

I ask Mom for the keys to her Prius, as Sunny took the Volkswagen Bug we share, and then head outside to start the car. My hands are already shaking when I turn the key in the ignition and I have no idea what kind of shape I'll end up being in when I reach my forbidden destination.

Yes, I'm heading to Club Fang. A venue I should definitely not be spending quality time at, seeing as it's totally a vampire hangout and I've just finished lecturing Sunny about how we must strive to live a vampire-free existence from here on out.

But how can I stay away? As much as I know I should. How can I go back on the promise I'd made to Jareth down in Hades after admitting I had to leave him? I'd promised to find him again and make him fall in love with me, no matter what I had to do. And I wasn't about to break that promise, even if the current Jareth in this time period has no idea I'd made it . . . or even who I am to begin with.

But whatever. I'll make it work. Someway. Somehow . . .

After parking in back, I pay my five dollars to the man standing at the door and head upstairs to the club itself. By day the space serves as a meeting spot for the Knights of Columbus, but you'd never know it now. The smoke machines work overtime and the strobe lights flash around the room as the walls reverberate from the heavy bass blasting from the speakers. The DJ is sitting behind a black cage, spinning my favorite Sisters of

Mercy tune, "Temple of Love," and the dance floor is packed with a mixture of mortals and vampires, all swaying intently to the beat. High above, TV screens soundlessly replay old vampire movie clips and the walls are draped with white sheets, flittering over strategically placed fans. God, I missed this place. It's like a real-life Fangtasia from *True Blood*, except for the absence of hot Sheriff Northman holding court in the back.

Which is fine by me. I've got another vampire in mind tonight.

I scan the crowd, my heart pounding wildly in my chest. It feels weird to have a beating heart at all, never mind one so active. I'd kind of forgotten what it was like to be human, after spending so many months undead. To feel so frail and weak. Even when I was a gimped vampire, because of the blood virus in my veins, I still felt a lot more, well, immortal, than I do now. At the moment I feel like a light wind could blow me over and a vampire could take me down with his little pinkie. It's a good thing I'm only here to flirt, not slay.

Speaking of flirting . . . My gaze falls upon a solitary figure in the center of the dance floor, illuminated by a single spotlight. My breath catches in my throat. Could it be?

Yes, I realize as I trace his silhouette with eager eyes. Without a shadow of a doubt.

It's Jareth.

He looks even more beautiful than I remembered him. So elegant, dressed in black leather pants, black boots, and billowing white shirt. His cheekbones are like cut glass and in the dim club lights his beautiful emerald eyes seem to glow in the dark. I stare in awe and delight, taking in his smooth, fluid movements on the dance floor, as graceful as the most graceful of cats. If he were a contestant on *Dancing with the Vamps*, he'd be a first-place winner for sure.

As I watch, it's all I can do to hang back. To stop myself from running up to him and accosting him with wild abandon, wrapping my arms around him and squeezing him tight as tears roll down my cheeks. But I check myself instead. If I want this to work—if I really want a second chance—I have to play it cool. To him, we'll be strangers, meeting for the first time. If I go all Stage Five Clinger on him right away, he'll go screaming off into the night and I'll lose my chance forever. Sure, it may take some time for him to warm up to me again, but I know if I do this right, it'll happen. After all, we're destined to be together. To become blood mates for all eternity. If I screw that up, well, I'm not sure how I'd be able to live with myself—by myself—forever.

My feet feel like lead as I force them to take steps onto the dance floor, dodging other dancers until I somehow manage to reach the center of the room. I'm two feet from him now and suddenly frozen into place. What do I say? What's my opening line? My tongue ties into knots and my brain refuses to work and I realize I should have come up with a better plan before I made my move. Or, you know, any plan at all.

I start to step backward, to retreat, but at that moment the DJ mixes into a rousing VNV Nation tune. The crowd roars in approval and an albino girl beside me, dressed from head to toe in Victorian steampunk, leaps in excitement, inadvertently shoving me straight into Jareth himself.

Well, that's one way to make an entrance. In fact, maybe this is just the opening I need. I'll fall into his strong arms, he'll reach out to catch me. He won't be able to help but feel the electric spark from our touch. And as he helps me gently back to my feet, he'll wonder why he has the strangest feeling that he knows me from somewhere. Somewhere deep in the recesses of time. Shocked, he'll grip me tighter, searching deep into my eyes, and he'll say—

"Do you mind removing your clodhopping boot from my foot?"

O-kay then. Not exactly the romantic speech I had in mind. Face flaming, I try to regain my balance without the help, I might add, of those aforementioned, strong, electricity-sparking arms. So much for chivalry. Or recognition. In fact, the only look he's giving me right now is one that suggests he's thinking about knocking me down all over again.

"Sorry about that," I say quickly, finding my center and brushing myself off. I look up at him, offering him my most charming smile. "It's crowded in here tonight, don't you think?"

"Not really," he says stiffly, before starting to turn away.

On instinct I grab his arm, not wanting to lose him now, now that I've got my opening, however small. He turns slowly back to me, giving my hand a deliberate look. I sheepishly let go of his shirt. This is not going well, is it?

"Um, do you come here often?" I blurt out, the only thing

that comes to my mind at short notice. Which just happens to be about the most unoriginal cliché thing that could come to mind in a circumstance like this. I'm so giving up my improv card.

He raises an eyebrow. "What does it matter to you if I do or I do not?"

Ugh. My smile falters at his rude reply. I guess I'd conveniently forgotten Jareth wasn't exactly Mr. Sunshine before he fell in love with me and learned it was okay to open up and share his feelings. In fact, now that I remember it, he could be a real jerk. And there was a time when I hated him more than anyone on earth, including that annoying girl from the T-Mobile commercials.

Of course nowadays I understand why he acted so emo. I mean, you try being all Pollyanna after losing your entire family to a Slayer Inc. attack. No wonder he refused a blood mate for so many years—not wanting to risk the pain of losing someone he loved all over again. He even refused blood donors, preferring to get his blood by mail order rather than risk becoming too close to another living soul who could someday die.

And so, until he met me, he chose to walk the world alone. A solitary, noble figure, rising above the petty trappings of relationships and—

"Hey, baby!"

My eyes widen as the most tacky Goth girl I've ever seen in the history of sight pushes me out of the way and throws her arms around Jareth, planting a sloppy black-lipsticked kiss on his lips. Whoa. Holy fangirl alert. I wait eagerly for Jareth to push her away. To tell her to get the hell out of his sight and then—

—kiss her back?!

"Hey, sweetie, I was wondering what happened to you," *my* boyfriend purrs to Miss Elvira, wrapping his arms around her and squeezing her tight. As he kisses the top of her head, it's all I can do to keep myself from screaming.

Okay, I admit it. I *can't* keep myself from screaming. In fact, I start screaming my head off, if you want to know the truth. But still! What would you do if you saw something like that? *Your* boyfriend, who always swore he hadn't been with anyone but you for a thousand years, hooking up with some random chick who is, I might add, completely not his type whatsoever?

Unfortunately, my screaming attracts the attention of the entire club. The DJ even turns off the music, probably thinking someone is getting drained dry on the dance floor. I clamp my mouth shut, my face burning like fire, and shrug.

"Um, sorry?"

"Who is this?" The girl demands, unwrapping herself from Jareth's arms and turning to look at me with narrow, piglike eyes. "And why is she staring at you, Jareth?" She gives me a condescending once-over, which is ridiculous, considering she's the one wearing last year's Hot Topic clearance threads.

Jareth rolls his eyes, looking bored. "Just some mortal who's evidently watched too many episodes of the *Vampire Diaries.*"

The girl sneers. "God, I *do* wish this ridiculous vampire trend would die already. It's getting *so* old."

Oooh I so want to punch that self-satisfied smirk off her

face. Almost as much I want to tell her that I liked vampires way before the whole *Twilight* phenomenon. Hell, I was reading Anne Rice and watching *Buffy the Vampire Slayer* in elementary school! How dare she try to play me up as some sparkly noob?

But I need to think bigger picture here. Like why the heck does Jareth have a girlfriend to begin with? I mean, sure, I hadn't technically met him yet the first time around—we didn't become acquainted for another month and a half, when I was assigned my first job for Slayer Inc. But still! He'd never once hinted at the time that he'd just gotten out of a serious relationship. If anything, he made it clear he'd been single for centuries.

But what can I do? Demand an explanation? Force him to explain why he never told me about a former girlfriend when, in his mind, we'd only met minutes before?

I force myself to face facts. As much as I'd like to know what the hell is going on, I realize this isn't the time or place to ask. If I suddenly start acting like a possessive freak, I'm only going to alienate him more. No, I need to bide my time instead, wait to get him alone. Then he'll likely be more amenable to explanation.

"Um, you can turn the music back on now," I inform the DJ, trying to keep the tremble from my voice. "Everything's cool." Luckily the DJ obliges, and a moment later Muse blasts through the club and everyone starts dancing again, drama forgotten.

Except Jareth and his hoochie mama GF, who are still standing there, staring at me.

"Well, I guess I'll, um, catch you later then," I stammer, feeling like I need to close this awkward conversation out somehow before vanishing into the night.

"I'll be waiting with bated breath," Jareth replies drolly. His stupid girlfriend chortles and it's all I can do to stop myself from drop-kicking her in the head. Instead, I force myself to take the high road, choosing to live to fight another day, turning and pushing my way through the crowd, ignoring the stares burning into my back as I head toward the exit.

I'm proud to say I manage to keep most of my tears at bay until I get into my mother's car and drive off into the night.

7

jump in the Prius and race home, trying and failing to obey most traffic laws. Which now is doubly risky, seeing as I no longer have that alluring vampire scent to charm my way out of a ticket, were I to be stopped by the police. But still, how can I rightly keep my mind on mundane things such as speed limits and stoplights when all I can I think about is Jareth sticking his tongue down another girl's throat?

As I pull onto our street, my mind flashes to those final moments I spent with Jareth down in the Underworld. When he took me into his arms as I cried and consoled me as I promised, over and over again, that I'd find him, no matter what it took. I remember him whispering in my ear, telling me not to worry. We were destined to be together, he said, and there was no way a pesky little thing like a time reset could ever come between us.

Was that Jareth—my Jareth—still there, hiding deep under that smug, arrogant, in-love-with-someone-tacky exterior? Or—and this was my biggest fear, deep down—had the strands of time already taken me down a different path? An alternate future where Jareth and I are no longer meant to be together?

It's all too much to contemplate. I pull into the driveway just in time for the tears to start all over again, blurring my vision and almost causing me to run into the garage. Salt tears, not the blood ones I'd gotten so used to crying over the last year as a vampire. A little less messy, but no more welcome, only serving to remind me that I am no longer that tough vampire, vampire-slayer girl that Jareth loved so much, but rather a weak, helpless mortal whose boyfriend is hooking up with another girl.

As I slink into the house, feeling as if my world has fallen apart, I see a light on in the kitchen. I follow it, surprised to find Sunny sitting at the kitchen table, eating a bowl of cereal. She looks up at me, an expression of relief written on her face.

"Where were you?" she asks. "I've been calling your cell all night."

"Sorry," I say, slumping down into a chair across from her. "I forgot it in the car."

Sunny squints at me. "Are you okay?"

"Sure, why wouldn't I be?" I demand, my tone more defensive than I mean it to be. I should have gone to the bathroom to wipe my face and put Visine in my eyes to stop the redness. After all, I so don't want to have to explain how I'd completely gone against what we'd agreed to on the very first night we'd agreed to it.

"Well, maybe it's just me, but I find most people who are okay don't usually have tears streaming down their cheeks and snot coming out of their nose."

Ugh. I swipe my nose with my sleeve before remembering how gross that must look to my sister. All these nasty slimy bodily functions I forgot about when I became a vampire. I mean, imagine spending nearly a year bathroom free and then suddenly having to remember to go every few hours . . . or else.

"It's just allergies. The pollen here is ridiculous."

"Rayne . . ." Sunny narrows her eyes and gives me a hard look. "I'm your identical twin. And neither one of us has ever suffered an allergy in our entire lives. It's part of the whole fairy gig. Remember how much money Mom saves on health insurance?"

"Fine," I retort, giving up the pretense. She's probably already figured it out anyway. "Jareth's dating someone else. Someone really tacky," I add, as if his having a cool girlfriend would be any better. But still! I want to assume he has some sort of taste in women—after all, he did pick me, right?

"And how do you know this, Miss Vampire Free, That's Me?" Sunny asks pointedly.

I sigh. "I went to Club Fang to go dancing," I confess. "How was I supposed to know that Jareth would be there? And with a tacky, nasty girlfriend, too." I scowl, thinking back at her vinyl pants and bat earrings.

"Well, for one thing it *is* his favorite hangout . . ."

Yeah, yeah. "Look," I say, deciding to come clean. "I tried to stay home. But I had to see him again. At least one more time.

Then I was going to leave him forever, I swear." I could feel the beads of sweat dripping down my forehead. God, it sucks to be a human. There are way too many ways to be caught lying.

Sunny purses her lips. "O-kay," she says slowly. "So you saw him. Are you ready to leave him forever now?"

I lean down, banging my head against the table mournfully. "No," I admit. "And I can't imagine I ever will be. I mean, one look and I was completely smitten all over again. Except for the fact that he was super-rude this time around."

"Um, if I remember right, he was super-rude the first time around as well," my sister reminds me.

"Yeah, but that was only because I was a member of Slayer Inc.," I protest. "The same organization that killed his family. This time he started hating on me for no reason whatsoever."

My sister raises an eyebrow.

"Okay, maybe there was a tiny reason. I tripped and stepped on his toes. But accidental toe-stepping shouldn't warrant full-on hate, should it? I mean, maybe mild dislike and annoyance. But you should have seen him. It was as if I'd burned up his favorite Batman shirt." I look up. "And did I mention he has a girlfriend? A tacky, nasty, disgusting girlfriend?"

"Hmm. Yes. Several times, in fact."

"I know, I know. But I can't help it. I mean, how would you like it if you went and found Magnus and he had a girlfriend in tow?" I sigh. "But, of course, you wouldn't go and do that. You're smarter than me and appreciate the second chance you've been given. You'd never go off and try to find Magnus after vowing to live a vampire-free . . ." I trail off, suddenly see-ing my sister for the first time. "Hang on a second. Is that my corset?"

Sunny's face turns bright red. "Um, maybe? Yeah?"

"Since when do *you* wear corsets?"

"Um . . ." She bites her lower lip. "Since *Easy A* was on HBO? Emma Stone rocked them so well, I thought I'd—"

"Sunshine McDonald. You went to see Magnus tonight!"

"No!" she cries, her eyes wide. "I just—"

"Just dressed up as me and attended my vampire-certification class," I conclude. "And here you had the nerve to go all Judge Judy on me for going to Club Fang."

Sunny stares down at her bowl of cereal.

"I knew it!" I cry, actually feeling kind of better knowing the truth. That I'm not the only weak McDonald twin after all. "He didn't have a surprise girlfriend, by any chance, did he? Like a really tacky, nasty, disgusting, hideous one?"

My sister shakes her head emphatically. As if *her* future boy-friend would never dream of cheating on *his* future love. "No," she says. "In fact, he was very sweet. Of course he thought I was you, I guess."

"Well, duh. You did wear my clothes."

"Which didn't impress him in the slightest, let me tell you," Sunny points out. She pauses, then adds, "Not to mention—how the heck do you scratch your bellybutton when you're wearing this thing?"

"You don't. You suffer for fashion," I reply curtly. "But let's not change the subject here, Sunny my girl. What happened at class? Did you let him bite you?" I study her neck closely, searching for marks or bruises. After all I sacrificed for her . . .

But my sister shakes her head. "No. No biting," she assures me. "Not even a practice one."

"You sound disappointed."

"No . . . well, not really." Sunny sighs. "Rayne, I've been thinking . . ."

I lean forward. "Yes?"

"Don't get me wrong. I appreciate all you did to get us back here and give us a second chance. And it's not like I suddenly want to become a vampire or anything. But, at the same time, do we really have to go all cold turkey on the entire other-world? I mean, look at us. Night number one and we've both epically failed to stay vampire free. What does that say about our chances for the future?"

"Well, I definitely wouldn't go to Vegas on the odds . . ."

"Exactly." Sunny nods. "And you know what? I don't necessarily think that's a bad thing. Do you?"

"But Sunny, look what happened the first time around!" I protest. "You were killed. Magnus was brought in for treason. The Blood Coven was kicked out of the Consortium. We don't want to start the chain of events all over again."

"Of course not," my sister agrees. "That would be crazy. But what if we could do something else? What if we could change things for the better? Figure out a way to not only save the Blood Coven and the rest of the Consortium from Pyrus's reign of terror but also get our boyfriends back?"

I frown. "It sounds good in theory, Sun, but how the heck are we going to make that happen? I mean, we essentially tried to do that already, and look what a disaster it turned out to be."

"But this time will be different," my sister says fervently, a strange light in her eyes.

"And how do we know that?"

Sunny smiles. "Because this time we know the future."

8

Sunny

Turns out, once you've made the decision to embark on a mission to save the world (once more with feeling), it's really tough to spend the entire next day locked away in a boring old high school. But unfortunately, since we can't clue Mom in to our superhero plans, she sees no reason why we can't make the bus on time. And I suppose there's not a ton we could do during the day anyway, seeing as all good vampires are fast asleep in their coffins during school hours.

Not to mention, as Rayne points out, you can't very well list *saving the world from a vampire apocalypse* on your college application as one of your extracurriculars. And now that she's no longer an immortal vampire with riches beyond belief, she's going to need to score a scholarship or two.

And so I'm forced to content myself to suffer through endless classes and tedious lunchtime talk, offering up a polite "Mm-hm" at all the appropriate pauses in conversation. But truth be told, if you asked me what my friends and teachers were going on about, I wouldn't have had a clue. All I can focus on is our master plan and how I'm going to get Magnus to go along with it, without spilling all the time-travel technicalities.

Rayne and I spent most of last night planning our strategy. Our idea is simple, really. I'll warn Magnus about Slayer Inc.'s threat to Lucifent's life and by doing so, earn the respect of him and the entire Blood Coven. Then, once they trust us, we can move on to the bigger fish we're hoping to fry—well, stake. Pyrus himself. It's perfect, really.

Finally the day ends and the sun goes down and Rayne and I head over to Club Fang, the scene of the crime, so to speak. As we get out of the car in the back parking lot, my eyes wander over to the simple wooden post where long ago (or next month, in this case) Magnus accidentally bit me and started my vampiric transformation. At the time, I'd been royally pissed off, not to mention horrified beyond belief. I mean, turning into a vampire one week before prom? So not cool.

But looking back on it now, after all of Magnus's and my adventures over the last year, that night will, without a doubt, go down as one of the most romantic in my entire life. I remember leaning against the post, my body pressed up against his, his lips brushing my neck—his fangs scraping my skin. It was the night I met my soul mate. A night that would change my life forever.

I still wonder sometimes what would have happened if we

hadn't been able to reverse the curse in time. What would it have been like to stay a vampire forever? Living as Magnus's blood mate for all eternity with nothing to tear us apart. Maybe things would have turned out differently. Maybe Bertha wouldn't have been able to kill me. Maybe Magnus and I could have fought against Pyrus and saved the Blood Coven right then and there. Maybe we could have lived happily ever after.

But I can't think of that now. It does no good. All I can do is focus on our current mission to change history for the better and hope for the best.

Rayne and I pay our cover and head upstairs into the club, pushing past all the weird Gothy patrons, all doing the same "foot stuck in the mud" dance on the dance floor. Seriously, dancing to Goth music seems like the dumbest thing ever to me. I mean, most of it's so freaking slow. How do you work up a good sweat just swaying your arms like that?

We leave the dance floor behind and head through a wooden door into a small coffeehouse at the back of the club. Or what appears, at first glance anyway, to be an establishment that serves coffee. The place actually specializes in a fine merlot that's not exactly fermented from grapes, if you get my meaning.

There, among a mess of motley patrons, sits Magnus, as expected, flanked by his two donor chicks, Rachel and Charity. Rayne nods to me and pushes me forward, then slinks back into the crowd, presumably to find Jareth. As I step toward the table, Charity recognizes me immediately from the night before and give out a delighted squeal before running over to hug me.

"How *are* you?" she asks, squeezing me with exuberance.

"You ran out so fast last night I didn't even get a chance to say good-bye. Is everything okay?" She peers at me with concerned eyes. "You haven't changed your mind, have you? I mean, about being a blood mate? Because Magnus really needs a good blood mate." She glances over at the vampire, a fond look in her eyes. "He's been kind of lonely, you know? Rachel and I have tried to keep him company over the last few years. But there's only so much we can do. He really needs that blood bond with an-other vampire. And you seem like such a nice girl. I think you'd be perfect for him." She gives me a worried smile. "So don't back out, okay? Don't break his heart."

I glance over at Magnus, my own heart suddenly feeling a little broken. I had no idea, that night he bit me, how much he'd been looking forward to having a blood mate of his own. And then I went and completely rejected him, demanding to be changed back into a human and treating him like a vile monster who tried to steal my soul. When all along, all he wanted was my heart.

Charity leads me over to the table, where Magnus is swish-ing around a goblet of wine. He looks up at me, his beautiful sapphire eyes lighting up as they fall upon me.

"You're back," he says, sounding surprised. "I thought when you left last night . . . before we could practice . . ."

"I know, I'm sorry," I say, pulling over a nearby chair. "I didn't mean to abandon you. There was just something I had to work out."

"I hope you were successful?"

I sit down in the chair, drawing in a breath. "Look, can we

talk?" I glance over at Rachel and Charity, watching with rapt eyes. "Alone?"

Magnus nods, then gestures to the donor chicks to make themselves scarce. Charity gives me a secretive wink while Rachel throws me a suspicious glare. I sigh and turn back to Magnus.

"So," I say, not sure where to begin. "I wanted to—"

Magnus raises a hand to stop me. "It's all right," he says. "I know what you're going to say and I understand."

"Um, I don't think you—"

"I felt you waffling at the church. And then you ran out before the practice bite." He gives me a sad smile. "I know you don't want to become a vampire. Not really, anyway. And I want you to know that that's okay with me. I mean, not that I don't want you. I've been waiting for a blood mate for some time now, after all. But I don't want you doing something you're going to regret. As I said last night, this is eternity we're talking about." He reaches out and places a hand on top of my own, sending a chill down my spine. "I will inform the council of your decision and they will send you a withdrawal form in the mail. You should expect to receive it between one to three—"

"Wait, wait, wait!" I cry. "That's not what I came here to say at all!"

Magnus drops my hand. He looks at me with a hope in his eyes that nearly kills me. "It's not?" he asks in a hoarse voice, as if he can scarcely believe his luck.

Gah. This is so hard. I mean, I don't want to give him false hope. But at the same time, we've got much more important things to discuss before we go down that whole blood-mate road. And if I tell him I'm backing out now, he'll never listen to what I have to say.

"No, I'm still planning on going through with it," I say, my lie tasting like sawdust in my mouth. I think back to all the times I yelled at him for lying to me. He'd tell me it was for my own good, something I could never understand. Now I think I'm starting to. "But right now we have more pressing matters." I lean over the table, lowering my voice to a whisper. "Your Master's life is in danger."

Magnus jerks to attention. "What did you say?"

"You heard me. Your Master. Lucifent. The little-boy vampire who sired you." I wonder how much I should reveal that I know. I want him to believe me, but I don't want him to get suspicious because I know too much. "There's a contract out on his head from Slayer Inc. One month from today they plan to send Bertha the Vampire Slayer into Blood Coven headquarters with a commission to dust him with her stake."

I pause, not daring to breathe as I wait for his reaction. Will he believe me? Everything we've planned up until this point in our little quest to save the future depends on it.

For a moment, Magnus is silent. Then he speaks. "How did you come across this information?" he asks quietly.

I bite my lower lip. How indeed? Obviously I can't tell him I'm a time traveler. That would just bring up too many unanswerable questions. But what else can I say? How would I know this information? "I can't reveal my sources," I say at last, deciding to plead the fifth. "But I can assure you the threat is very real."

Magnus frowns, staring down into his glass of wine. I can almost see the thoughts whirling around in his head like a prairie tornado. He wants to believe me, even though he thinks what I'm saying is completely absurd.

"Look, I'm going to be a member of the Blood Coven soon," I remind him. "And the last thing I want is for something to happen to our fearless leader before I even get a chance to join." I look at him pleadingly. Silently begging him to believe me.

He pushes back his chair abruptly, rising to his feet. "Come."

"Um, what?" I squint up at him, confused. Not exactly the reaction I was expecting. "Come where?"

"Lucifent must be informed of this threat," Magnus says. "I will bring you to him so you can tell him what you know."

Wait, he wants *me* to tell him? "Oh. I don't know if that's such a good idea . . ." I stammer. After all, though I'd only met the Blood Coven Master once, mere minutes before his death, let's just say he wasn't as cuddly or cute as he appears to be. In fact, now that I think about it, he was kind of mean. "Can't you just, you know, warn him yourself?" In my head I can hear Rayne calling me a wimp, but I push the thought from my mind.

"I could," Magnus replies. "But I'm guessing he'd prefer to hear about his impending demise straight from the source."

"Even if the source in question is an inconsequential mortal girl he doesn't know from a hole in the wall?" I know I'm grasping at straws here, but I can't help it. "Wouldn't he prefer to hear it from his own progeny, vampire to vampire and all that?"

"You're going to be a full member of the Blood Coven and my blood mate in one month," Magnus points out. "I see no reason why he shouldn't respect you and hear you out."

Sigh. I'm not going to get out of this, am I? I just have to pray Lucifent's in an indulgent mood and not into killing messengers and such. "Fine," I say reluctantly. "Lead the way."

As I rise from my seat, I expect Magnus to lead me outside into his BMW and drive me over to Blood Coven HQ in St. Patrick's Cemetery. But it turns out Lucifent evidently enjoys a little night life himself because instead I'm brought back through the dance floor of Club Fang, through a locked door at the other end of the hall, and behind a red velvet curtain, into a small, stark room I've never seen before. There, two vampires stand guard before a plain wooden door.

"We're here to see Lucifent," Magnus informs the guards.

The two vampires look at one another, then turn back to Magnus. "The Master is at dinner. He asks not to be disturbed."

Phew. "Oh well, we'll have to tell him some other time, I guess," I say quickly, relieved to have an out. "Or, you know, you can tell him when you see him, Magnus. At some point when I'm probably not hanging around . . ."

Magnus ignores me. "This girl has vital information regarding the Master's safety," he insists, giving the guards a steely look. "I expect he will want to be interrupted to hear her tale."

"Fine." The guard on the left turns and opens the door behind him just a crack, slipping through and yanking it shut before I can get a good peek inside. We wait in awkward silence, the second guard giving us a squirrelly look. A moment later the door opens again. But it's not the guard—or Lucifent—who steps into the room.

"Jareth!" I cry out in surprise before I can remember I'm not supposed to know the vampire in question. "Um," I say quickly. "That's your name, right?"

He stops short as he sees me and a flush of anger crosses his face. "You again!" he growls. "I thought I told you to leave me alone!"

Uh-oh. I glance at Magnus, who's now looking from me to Jareth and back again, confusion in his eyes. What did Rayne go and do now? I thought it would be safe to leave her alone for a minute or two, but evidently not so much.

And unfortunately Jareth's not finished. "I told you. I don't want to talk. I don't want to take a midnight walk on the beach. And I certainly don't want to partake in a quick juicing of your jugular." He bares his fangs at me, as if to try to scare me off. "I'm a very busy vampire, I'll have you know, and I don't have time for any of your shenanigans."

"Jareth, I think you have this girl mistaken for someone else," Magnus cuts in. "This is Rayne McDonald. My future blood mate."

"Well, your future blood mate has just spent the last fifteen minutes trying to make me fall in love with her," Jareth says with a scowl. "Telling me we're soul mates from another life and that I should dump my girlfriend and hook up with her instead."

Oh, Rayne . . . So not in the plan!

"That's impossible," Magnus protests. "She has been with me this entire time."

"Are you calling me a liar?" Jareth demands, his face turning purple.

"Well, if the cape fits . . ."

Jeez Louise. "Um, hello?" I interject. "I can explain?"

The two vampires turn to look at me. I draw in a breath and address Jareth first. "You have me mistaken for my twin sister. She's the one who wants to hook up with you." Then I turn to Magnus. "And I'm your blood mate." Well, sort of anyway. It's going to be very confusing if he keeps thinking of me as Rayne. But how can I explain our little switcheroo? It'll only make things even more bewildering—if that's possible at this point.

"Your blood mate?" Jareth snorts. "Wow. They must really be scraping the bottom of the barrel these days." He gives me a scornful look, as if I'm gum he found on the bottom of his shoe. *Nice one, jerk. Way to go judging me 'cause you don't like my twin.*

Luckily I have my own personal knight in shining armor by my side, ready to defend me. "Jareth!" Magnus cries in a shocked and angry voice. "This girl has done nothing to deserve your disrespect. You will apologize to her and—"

"Guys, guys!" I interrupt. "We don't have time for this!" Though, to be honest, I wish we did, as it's more than a little nice to watch Magnus stick up for me, not even knowing who I really am. "I have to gain an audience with Lucifent and inform him about the threat on his life. That's all that matters right now."

Jareth narrows his eyes. "And where, might I ask, is this so-called threat coming from?"

"Slayer Inc."

"I see." The vampire general purses his lips. "And your proof?"

Er . . . Oh crap. I should have known he'd ask for that.

"I, um, don't really have any?" I stammer. "But you should take me seriously. I know what I'm talking about."

Jareth shakes his head. "Do you know how many false threats we get on the Master's life every day? I have no time to follow up on each and every one of them. And the last thing the Master needs is to be bothered by some crazy, ranting mortal with an even crazier sister who has no proof to back up her claim. He's got a very busy schedule, you know."

"Well, I can assure you his calendar will be completely clear next month, after he's been staked through the heart," I dare to say. "But, sadly, then it'll be too late to warn him."

Jareth rolls his eyes. "Come back with proof," he says. "And maybe I will see about granting you an audience. Until then, please go away. And tell your sister to go away, too. Magnus, here, may be blinded by your beauty, but I know your kind all too well. You're trouble with a capital T, and I want nothing to do with either of you."

And with that, he storms into the back room, slamming the door shut behind him. "Whatever," I mutter, annoyed by the whole thing at this point. Lucifent doesn't want to be saved? Fine by me. We should have just left things well enough alone, I guess, and not tried to go out of our way to save the future.

I turn and stomp down the hall, heading back to the dance floor to find my sister.

But before I can open the door, I feel a hand on my shoulder, turning me around. Magnus has followed me down the corridor, an apologetic look on his face. "I'm sorry," he says. "Jareth means well. And he's very loyal. But he can be kind of . . . rough around the edges at times."

"I know," I say with a sigh. "I mean, I've heard," I correct quickly, catching Magnus's look. "I mean, he seems that way. To be honest, I'm not sure what my sister sees in him." I shrug. "But whatever. I've done my best. If your coven refuses to take me seriously, then there's really nothing I can do." I start for the door again, but Magnus stops me.

"Tell me," he says in a low voice. "Is Lucifent truly in danger?"

"God, do you think I would be bothering with all of this if he wasn't?" I demand. "I mean, no offense, but I have better things to do than get humiliated by arrogant, self-serving vampires. For example, I haven't even begun to study for my chem test tomorrow."

"Then I believe you," Magnus says simply.

"You do?"

He gives me a rueful smile. "You're my blood mate. Why would you lie?"

I can think of a million reasons, actually. But I'm not going to mention any of them right now. Instead, I'm just going to enjoy the fact that he's willing to take me at face value, without demanding any proof.

"Except we're going to need some proof," he adds gently. "I mean, if you want the others to take you seriously, that is."

Sigh.

"But I can help you get it," he adds. "If you know where to look."

I raise my eyebrows in surprise. This, I wasn't expecting.

"Okay," I say, nodding, a plan forming in my mind. "Well, from what I understand, Slayer Inc. is as big on the red tape as you guys are," I muse aloud. "And they're bound to have done some kind of investigation. Maybe they've even put together an official commission." I think back to some of Rayne's past slayer assignments. She always got a folder with background information and photos, along with the slay order. It made sense to think they'd have created one for Lucifent, as well.

"Of course," Magnus agrees. "And if we could somehow find this order and bring it back to show Lucifent . . ."

"Then he'd have to take us seriously," I conclude. "And maybe we can still stop this murder before it's too late."

"Well, then what are we waiting for?" the vampire says with a smile. "Let's go get our proof."

9

My heart pounds as Magnus pulls the BMW over to the side of the road, just down the street from the spooky old manor at the edge of town that serves as Slayer Inc.'s secret headquarters. (Though evidently not *so* secret, since the vampire knows exactly how to get there, without so much as a Google Map.) The whole trip I'm furiously texting my sister, whom we left behind at Club Fang, to get any and all information she can give us about breaking into this place, seeing as she used to frequent it quite a bit, back in her slayer days. Thankfully she's able to give me some alarm codes and information on the layout, so we won't be completely on a fool's mission.

"I can't believe we're doing this," I hiss as we slip out of the car and head down the road toward the mansion. It's pitch-dark, and unlike Magnus, I don't have vampire night vision. So

I clutch his arm and allow him to lead me off-road and through the woods. It'd be kind of romantic, if only my heart weren't sounding like an 808 drum in my chest. After all, I know from personal experience that Slayer Inc. is no organization to mess around with. And I doubt if I go and get myself killed a second time around, Hades will grant another do-over.

"Well if we're going to find proof, this is where it'll be," Magnus whispers back, gently guiding me over a small bridge that spans a stream. He's so close I can feel his breath at the back of my neck, which sends a shiver down my spine. I can't help but wonder if he's feeling the same attraction to me as I am to him. I mean, he was attracted to me the first time around, so I must still be his type, right? Plus the fact that I'm no longer Gothed out to the max has to score me at least a few extra cuteness points.

I shake my head. What am I thinking? I need to concentrate on my mission here, not lapse into girly-girlness. Distractions will only get us killed. There will be time for flirtation later, after we save Lucifent.

I start to feel like a secret super-spy as we stealthily approach the mansion from behind. We locate the back door that my sister had texted me about. Hands shaking, I manage to type in the alarm code she gave me, praying it works. I can see Magnus's questioning look, and I know he's wondering where I acquired such proprietary information, but in the spirit of being silent so as not to get caught, he luckily doesn't ask.

Once we're inside, I glance down at my phone again, going through Rayne's detailed instructions on how to get to Vice

President Teifert's office. If the slay order exists, it'll probably be there. I motion for Magnus to follow me down a long, cobweb-filled hallway, praying we don't run into any huge spiders on the way. Seriously, for a multinational organization, they really need to cough up a little more cash for proper custodial services.

As I step on a loose floorboard, a loud groan echoes through the house, causing me to nearly jump out of my skin. Though my sister swore to me that no one stays in this place overnight and they rely on an alarm system rather than real-life security guards, I still get the creepy feeling that someone's there, watching us in the darkness, waiting for the right moment to pounce. I cuddle up a little closer to Magnus, just in case, as we continue down the hall.

We take a left, then a right, and then another left, and by the time we reach the end of the fourth corridor, I'm feeling kind of lost. All the doors look exactly alike in the darkness and I have no idea how we're going to figure out which one belongs to Teifert.

"I think this is it," Magnus points out suddenly, gesturing to yet another nondescript door as we turn the corner.

I squint at the door in question, then back at him. "How do you know? It looks like every other door we've passed for the last ten minutes." I frown. "You don't have X-ray vision, do you?" Sure, he's never hinted about anything like that before, when listing his vampire megapowers. But maybe it's because he wants to keep that particular ability on the down-low. I mean, it's one thing to brag about super strength or speed. But admitting you can steal a peek at your girlfriend's Vicky Secret anytime you like could put you in a rather awkward position with the girlfriend in question.

"Um, no," he says with a small chuckle. "I merely have regular vision, which I used to read the nameplate located on the side of the door."

Oh. Right. My eyes fall upon the brass plate affixed to the wall next to the door. Duh. For a secret super-spy on a mission to save the world, I really need to work on my basic skills of observation. I guess it's a good thing Magnus decided to tag along.

Here goes nothing. I wrap my hand around the doorknob and turn.

Unfortunately, it doesn't budge.

"Hmm," I whisper, searching the nearby wall for some kind of security panel but coming up empty. This lock appears to be more the old-fashioned type, needing a physical key. "Can you break it down, perhaps?" Not exactly subtle, but I can't see any other options.

Magnus gestures for me to step aside. "Allow me," he whispers. But instead of heaving his body against the door, he retrieves a small bag out of his pants pocket and kneels before the doorknob, pulling out what appears to be a silver bobby pin and sliding it into the lock.

I watch him work, amazed. "Since when do you pick locks?" I can't help but ask. All this time I knew him and he'd never mentioned this particular skill set.

"Since the seventeen hundreds," he replies, keeping his eyes focused on his work. "Back then there was no Consortium or covens to unite vampires and keep them in the lifestyle they are now accustomed to." He pulls out another pin from the bag and inserts it in the lock. "So we had to get creative if we wanted to survive." He gives me a quick glance before going back to his work. "Just be thankful you'll never have to live in a world like that. The forming of the Consortium is the best thing that ever happened to vampires."

I frown, getting an icky feeling from the whole "rah-rah Consortium" speech. After all, this is the same Consortium that, in my time, is trying to take over the world. The same Consortium that has accused Magnus of treason and cast out his coven, simply because he spoke out against their dictator of a leader and asked for a return of democracy. Not exactly the kind of organization that makes you feel all warm and fuzzy inside.

But the problem is, I realize, none of this has happened yet, and thus, Magnus is still naively loyal to the group. Heck, it took him a ridiculously long time to see the truth the first time around. And now I'm going to have to start from scratch if I want him on my side to help us take Pyrus down.

But first things first. Save Lucifent now. Prove I know what I'm talking about. Then maybe they'll listen to me about the rest.

Magnus rises to his feet. "Got it."

I give him two enthusiastic thumbs up. "Thank God for your misspent vampire youth," I tease. He flashes me a bashful grin, then grabs the knob, turns it, and pushes open the door.

CREAK!

I cringe. Turns out, even if you are wise enough to go about picking locks instead of using vampire strength to break down the door, if the door in question hasn't been WD-40'ed in the last fifty years, it's not going to exactly work in your silent favor. In fact, I couldn't imagine a louder noise than if we'd detonated some C-4 to blow the door in. If anyone really is here, lurking in the dark, they now know without a doubt they've got company.

"Let's get this and get out of here quick!" I urge.

Magnus doesn't need a second invitation. I follow him into the office and head straight for the desk at the center of the room, rummaging through drawers as fast as my hands will let me, searching for our proof. Magnus takes the file cabinet at the far wall, dumping out drawers and scanning documents with super-speed, all while keeping a watchful eye on the door.

"Look!" I cry, grabbing a folder marked *Lucifent* from the pile. Magnus drops the papers he'd been rummaging through and joins me at the desk. With trembling hands, I peel open the folder and examine the contents inside. Could this be our smoking gun?

"Hell," Magnus swears under his breath, evidently a faster reader than me. "You were right. They really are planning to go through with it." He grabs the folder from my hands and slaps it shut. "Let's go," he says. "We have to get this to Lucifent. Pronto."

"I don't think so," snarls a female voice.

I shriek as a figure steps out of the darkness and stands, silhouetted in the doorway. Oh God. We've been caught. And not only caught, but caught by the worst person possible to get caught by.

Bertha the Vampire Slayer. My murderer.

10

Bertha the Vampire Slayer. I'd almost forgotten what she looked like, pre–extreme makeover. But the sight of her now brings it all rushing back to me. A pockmarked face, greasy blond hair, beady little pig eyes, and a body smooshed into tight black leather three sizes too small. The fat oozing out the sides makes me more than a little nauseated. Or maybe it's the sight of the wooden stake, holstered at her side.

"Who are you?" she growls. "And what do you think you're doing here?"

My mind races for an answer that will save us. I do not want to face her in a full-on fight after the last time. Then I remember I'm still technically posing as my sister. Maybe that can work out to our advantage.

"My name is Rayne McDonald," I declare with as much

bravado as I can muster on short notice. "I am a vampire slayer, like you, and I have apprehended a prisoner." I turn to gesture to Magnus, at the same time trying to wink at him without Bertha seeing so he'll understand this is only a ruse. The last thing I need is for him to believe me and try to take both of us on.

Luckily he seems to get it, bowing his head and looking all submissive-like.

Bertha screws up her face. "That's impossible. There's only one girl born in each generation, destined to slay all the—"

"Save it, you Buffy wannabe," I interrupt. "Do you really think Slayer Inc. wouldn't have a backup stashed away for emergencies? Especially when their so-called destined slayer can't seem to keep her cholesterol levels in check." I give her a pitying smile. "I hate to tell you, Bertha my girl, but you're not exactly the special snowflake you think you are." I grab Magnus roughly by the arm, praying he'll continue to play along. "Now if you'll excuse me, I have to process my prisoner." I make a move toward the door.

For a moment Bertha is silent and I start thinking we're actually going to get away with this nonsense. But just as we reach the door, she leaps in front of us, blocking our path. "If you really are a slayer," she says, "then you'll know the secret password."

Oh crap. Rayne didn't tell me there was a secret password. Or maybe there isn't. Maybe she's trying to fake me out or something.

"Please. There is no password," I decide to try, seeing as

even if there is one, I don't have a clue as to what it could be. "Now get out of my face before I report you to Teifert for obstruction of slayer justice."

Bertha calmly stretches out her arm, reaching for a button on the wall. As she depresses it, a steel door comes crashing down over the only exit and an alarm starts blaring. Uh-oh. Guess I guessed wrong on the password thing.

A computerized female voice comes over the airwaves. "Intruder alert. Intruder alert."

I glance over at Magnus. So much for bluffing our way out of here. Now our only option is to fight. As Bertha lunges at me, I leap aside, dodging her attack while my eyes scan the room desperately for some kind of weapon to even the playing field. But, for a vice president of a vampire-slaying organization, Teifert seems decidedly understocked in the arsenal department, with not even a spare stake to be seen.

Bertha whirls around, her face a mask of anger as she winds up for round two. But this time Magnus is ready for her. He hurdles in front of me, his fangs clicking into place as he grabs her roughly by the shoulders.

"Oh, you want to play, too, vampire?" she snarls.

Quick as lightning she flips herself backward, freeing herself from Magnus's grip and launching to the other side of the office. For someone so skinny-challenged, the girl can really move when she wants to. Once she's out of fangs' way, she whips out her stake, lunging forward at Magnus with a screeching battle cry.

I stare in horror as she rushes him, déjà vu hitting me hard and fast. This was exactly how she took out Lucifent. Quick, decisive, and without a single line of Buffy-esque banter. Just charge, stake, and poof! No more Blood Coven Master.

I can't let that happen to Magnus.

I step in, shoving the vampire out of her path as Bertha brings her stake down. The sharp wood drives into my forearm instead, causing me to squeal in pain. I may not be a vampire who implodes from a stake to the heart, but let me tell you, it still doesn't feel like a day at the beach to have a piece of wood jammed into one's flesh. Not to mention the major sliver potential.

Bertha, evidently startled by my sudden heroics (after all, what vampire slayer jumps in to save a vampire?) seems confused, staring down at the stake embedded in my arm. Before she can manage to rip it out, I take advantage, slamming my fist into her face as hard as I can. Unfortunately I'm no prizefighter, so I'm not a hundred percent sure my valiant efforts will even leave a bruise, but I feel pretty cool for landing my first punch, nonetheless. If only Rayne were here to see me now.

Bertha staggers backward, her hand flying to her face. Magnus springs into action, moving so fast I can barely track it. Gotta love the vampire super-speed. He tackles Bertha, bringing her crashing to the floor, using his weight to pin her down.

I yank the stake out of my arm, trying to ignore the gush of blood that splashes from the open wound onto the floor.

"Go!" Magnus cries, struggling to hold down the writhing slayer beneath him. "Run! Get out of here!"

I have to admit, it's good advice. But at the same time there's no way I'm abandoning my boyfriend to a slayer. Sure, he appears to have the upper hand now. But I know how slippery Bertha can be. And if I did jump ship and something ended up happening to him? I'd never be able to forgive myself.

Sure enough, a moment later, Magnus screams in pain, stumbling backward, freeing Bertha from his hold. At first I can't figure out what happened, but then I see the knife sticking out of his gut. A knife that I'm pretty sure, from his reaction, is made of pure silver. Just as iron is poison to some fairies, so silver is to vampires. Bertha rises to her feet, straddling Magnus's prostrate frame, her back to me.

"Time to die," she growls, reaching for the knife.

Rage explodes inside me. Once again the slayer has gone too far. With a bellowing, *Braveheart*-esque shriek, I charge, slamming the stake into Bertha's back. Again, I know it probably won't do any permanent damage, but a piece of wood stuck in your back is a piece of wood, when all's said and done.

She screams in pain, whirling around to face me, her beady eyes bulging with anger. "Oh, I'm sorry," she says. "Did you want to go first?" She stalks toward me, her steps eating up the room with a frightening pace. I back up, now weaponless, until I'm flush against the wall. I steal a glance at Magnus, hoping for a last-minute rescue, but something tells me that's not going to happen, what with him thrashing on the floor in pain and all.

Bertha reaches me. I try to shove her away, but she's too strong, wrapping her meaty hands around my neck and squeezing tight, cutting off my air passageways. I latch on to her hands with my own, desperate to pull them away as I struggle for breath. But I can't seem to pry them off, no matter how hard I try. My vision starts to blur. My lungs are empty. Could this be it? Could this be game over once again? That would be so unfair, to allow Bertha to kill me a second time.

"Wait!" a male voice booms. As Bertha releases her grip in surprise, I glance over to the doorway. The metal wall has lifted and standing there in a bathrobe and bunny rabbit slippers is none other than Vice President Teifert himself.

What, is everyone having a Slayer Inc. sleepover or something?

Teifert steps calmly into the room, as if all hell isn't currently breaking loose. He presses the alarm button on the wall and the sirens fade to oblivion. The room is now eerily silent as he surveys the scene.

"What is the meaning of this?" he asks at last, sounding a little weary.

"This girl," Bertha spits out, glaring at me. "She says she's a vampire slayer. But I caught her and her little vampire boyfriend breaking and entering into your office. I felt it was my duty to stop them." She looks at Teifert, a desperate plea for approval written on her pockmarked face. For a top vampire slayer, she's got more than a few insecurity issues.

Teifert steps over to Magnus, who is still lying bleeding on the floor. He yanks the knife from his side, and Magnus gasps in agony as it's ripped free. "I truly thought better of you, Magnus," Teifert says in a soft voice.

"Well, I thought better of you," Magnus growls. "But this paper seems to suggest otherwise." With a shaky hand, he gestures to the folder with Lucifent's slay order, which has spilled out onto the floor. "You're supposed to protect and serve," he says. "But all I see is an intent to kill."

"We have our reasons for that," Teifert says stiffly, his face turning red as a tomato. He grabs the folder and stuffs the papers back into it. "Not that it's any of your business."

"He's my sire," Magnus heaves. I can tell it's taking a lot of effort to talk. I wonder why he's not healing. Maybe the silver in his bloodstream is preventing it? If only I could get him out of here, get him to his blood donors for a proper transfusion . . .

"Your sire, yes. And your current Master. But there's more to Lucifent than you know. And he must be brought to justice before it's too late."

"I won't let you slay him," Magnus insists. "Kill me instead."

Teifert sighs. "If only you could understand," he says. "We're doing this to save your coven. With Lucifent at the helm, you're all in danger." He pauses, then adds, "Along with the entire human race."

"What?" I cry, before I can help myself. "But I thought you killed—er, I mean are planning to kill—Lucifent because he's a child vampire, which is against your laws." Oh God, was there something else? Something we don't know about the vampire leader that Slayer Inc. does? Something bad?

Teifert turns to me. "While we don't exactly endorse the idea of children being turned into creatures of the night, we certainly wouldn't advocate their murder—not to mention disruption of an entire vampire coven's governing body—for that simple reason alone. This is the twenty-first century, after all."

Uh-oh.

"And if we did for some ridiculous reason, wouldn't we have seen fit to have done the deed years ago?" Teifert continues to reason, pacing the room from one side to the other. "It's not as if he hasn't been a child vampire for several millennia, you know."

Ugh. Good point. Why didn't Rayne and I think of that?

Teifert's gaze settles on me. "And you," he says. "What are you even doing here? This is not your battle to fight. You should leave now." He gestures to the door. "Leave and forget all you've seen here tonight. We'll talk in the morning at school."

I bite my lower lip. His offer is more than a bit tempting. Walk out the door and have it all forgiven. Forget everything that we tried to do, which maybe, judging from what Teifert is hinting at, may not have been a good idea to begin with.

But then I catch Magnus's desperate look out of the corner of my eye. It's my fault he's in this mess. If I leave now, I'm basically abandoning him. Betraying him in his hour of need. If I walk out the door, it'll be over between us forever. I'll never gain his trust. I'll never gain his love.

So instead, I cross my arms over my chest. "I'm Magnus's intended blood mate," I inform Teifert staunchly, praying I'm not making a huge mistake. "His battles are my battles. And I won't abandon him to Slayer Inc."

Teifert sighs again, running a hand through his hair, as if weary of the world. "Wonderful," he mutters, walking over to the desk and tossing the folder back inside. "This is just what I needed to cap off my already terrific day."

"Can I kill them now?" Bertha asks eagerly.

"No," Teifert says. He surveys the two of us with solemn eyes. "Despite what these two seem to believe, we're not monsters here at Slayer Inc. and we don't go around murdering vampires and humans for no just cause."

Bertha scowls. Evidently she doesn't agree with the current administration's policies on senseless monster murder.

"So, um, then can we go then?" I ask, daring to hope for a split second. Will he let us just walk out of here? Can I get Magnus to his donors before it's too late?

But Teifert dashes that idea with a quick shake of his head. "I'm sorry. You know too much," he says, addressing Magnus more than me. "Making you a danger to your people." He sheathes the dagger and slips it into his pocket. "Until we finish this order of business I'm afraid we can't let you free."

11

'm sure there are very few dungeons, if any, in this world that could be mistaken for five-star hotels. But, I have to say, the Slayer Inc. dungeon is particularly nasty. First of all, it probably hasn't been cleaned since the Reagan era. And the walls and floors are covered in bloodstains. But the worst part? Since vampires don't have the same kind of bodily functions as humans, there's not a toilet to be found. And I'm starting to deeply regret that Big Gulp I drank on the way to Club Fang.

Magnus collapses onto the lumpy, stained cot at the back of the cell, groaning softly to himself. He's ripped off his shirt and pressed the cloth to the wound, which still isn't healing as fast as it should be. He's lost a ton of blood already and I'm starting to get more than a little concerned as a crimson stain starts seeping into the cloth.

"What was I thinking?" he laments, staring up at the ceiling. "Coming here was a fool's mission. And now I'm stuck here, helpless, while Slayer Inc. goes to kill my Master."

"Why do they want to kill Lucifent?" I ask. "Do you know?"

"Because they're an evil organization with a lust for power?"

I wrinkle my nose. "But they aren't. They're peacekeepers, for the most part. At least the U.S. chapter. If they say Lucifent is a danger to the coven, they must have a reason." I pace the cell back and forth. "Do you know what he could be involved in?"

"Lucifent doesn't share his plans with me," Magnus says with a shrug. "If anyone would know, it'd probably be Jareth, him being general of the army and all. If only we could contact him. At least to let him know he should beef up his security team and protect the Master."

"Yeah, well, if he had believed me in the first place, this wouldn't be an issue," I say absently, though half of me now wonders if Jareth's disbelief might not have been a good thing after all. What if Teifert was telling the truth—that there really was another reason Lucifent needed to be slain, besides the fact that he was a child vampire? Here we are, trying to change history for the better; what if we almost made things much, much worse?

I shake my head, telling myself it doesn't matter in the end. We're stuck in jail. Bertha and Teifert have gone on to expedite the Master's murder. So things will end up working out exactly how they did the first time around, give or take a few weeks. Maybe it's for the best we were caught after all.

Except for Magnus's wound. His shirt is now drenched in blood.

"That doesn't look good," I say worriedly. "We need to do something about that."

He grimaces. "I'm fine. I'm a vampire. I'll heal."

"The knife that cut you was silver plated. The cut won't heal fast enough and you're losing too much blood. You need a transfusion or something."

"Good idea," he says sarcastically. "Why don't you text my blood donors? Tell them to swing by the dungeon for a quick bite." He winces in pain.

I let out a slow breath, sinking down beside him on the bed. I can't bear to see him in such agony. Not to mention, even if he does manage to survive, there is no way we can stage any prison break with him so weakened.

I rise to my feet, walking over to the cell door, grabbing the bars in my hands. Peering left and right, I search for a guard or someone else in charge. But the place is deserted.

"Hello?" I cry. "Anyone there? We need some blood down here. Now!"

My demands echo through the hallways but there's no answer.

"Hello," I try again, not ready to give up. "Anyone? Please?"

Magnus waves a weak hand in my direction, beckoning me away from the bars. "It's no use," he says. "Even if there were someone there to help, it's not like they would. I'm better off to them when I'm weak and vulnerable."

"Right." I plop back down onto the bed, dropping my head

into my hands, feeling helpless and weak. I stare at our cell phones, sitting on a nearby table, outside the cell—so close and yet so far away. If only I had been gifted with those mental telepathy powers that twins always seem to have in the movies. Then I could summon my sister and let her know the mess we're in.

"Why did you stay?" Magnus asks suddenly.

I lift my head, turning to the vampire in surprise. "What?"

"You could have left. When I had Bertha pinned. And again when Teifert told you to walk out the door. Why didn't you?"

Why didn't I indeed? Maybe I could have gone and gotten help. But still . . .

"What was I supposed to do? Just abandon you here with a slayer who wanted you dead?"

"Well, yes," Magnus says simply. "Actually that was exactly what you were supposed to do."

"Well, I couldn't," I reply, trying to keep my voice emotionless. "Like I said, you're my intended blood mate. I couldn't simply walk away and . . ." I trail off as a lump forms in my throat and tears threaten my eyes. He has no idea what I would have gone through to save him. Heck, I would have gladly given up my own life to let him live. But to him, I'm practically a stranger who owes him nothing. In his mind, there's no real reason I should have stayed behind.

I feel a hand on my shoulder. Magnus has managed to rise to a sitting position and is peering at me with large, beautiful eyes. "You willingly risked your life to save me," he whispers.

"No one has ever done that for me before." His voice is full of wonder, and it breaks my heart to hear the loneliness creep in at the edges.

"Yeah, well, get used to it," I mutter, trying and failing to sound gruff. "After all, you're stuck with me for a very long time."

He smiles shyly. "I like the sound of that," he says. Then he frowns. "Of course, first I have to live through the night." He collapses back onto the bed, pressing the blood-soaked shirt against his wound. I watch him, everything inside me aching to see him in such pain. If only there were a way I could—

I swallow hard, suddenly realizing exactly what I need to do.

"I've got an idea," I tell him, pulling up my sleeve and holding my wrist out to him. I'm not sure exactly how this is done, but I remember this is what Sookie did during an episode of *True Blood.* "Here."

He cocks his head in question. "Here what? Your hand is empty."

"Actually it's full of delicious, nutritious O negative."

I wait for his eyes to light up as he realizes what I'm saying. Instead all I get is a frown. "I don't think that's a good idea."

"Of course it is," I insist. "In fact, it's a very good idea. The best idea possible at this point in time. And probably the only one. I mean, let's be practical here. You're injured. You need blood to heal. I've got plenty to spare."

"But we're not supposed to take blood from our blood

mates until the official biting ceremony," he protests. "It's against the rules."

Oh, Magnus and his sense of propriety. It'd be cute if it weren't so life-threatening in this case. "Well, look at it this way," I say. "There won't be a biting ceremony if you don't last the night. So I think maybe a special dispensation is in order." I drag a fingernail down my wrist, trying not to wince as I draw a drop of blood. I can see the hunger on Magnus's face as the red liquid drips down onto the stained cot. "Come on," I urge. "Sweet, syrupy blood. You know you want it. What could go wrong?"

"I could lose control and drain you dry," Magnus points out.

Touché. "Well," I say, pushing all doubts from my head. "I trust you. You're going to be my blood mate, after all. Just take what you need and leave me a little for the ride home and we'll be all set."

He chuckles softly. "All right," he says. "If you're sure . . ."

"Positive."

I watch as, hands trembling, he carefully draws my wrist to his mouth, soft lips brushing against my delicate flesh and causing an involuntary shiver. I swallow hard, bracing myself for the next part. The part that isn't so soft and sweet.

"You did watch the instructional video after I left, right?" I can't help but ask. "And you practiced on the dummy?"

I can feel his smile against my skin. "Don't worry. I'm fully licensed to bite," he quips, sending chills down my spine as his mouth moves against my skin. "This won't hurt a bit."

"Well then, let's get this show on the road." Before I lose my nerve.

And so he does. And, as his fangs sink down, breaking the skin and piercing my veins, instead of pain, I feel only pleasure. A warm, sweeping sensation like an ocean wave, washing over me, engulfing me entirely. And as the blood flows from me to him, I feel our minds dancing with one another, my essence flowing into him, giving him new life and new power. It's an exhilarating feeling, to say the least. So beautiful, I can't help but wonder why we never did this before. It could have brought us so close, especially on those days we felt so apart.

But just as I'm surrendering to the sensation, Magnus rips his mouth away, his face clouded with confusion. As he stares at me, as if I'm some sort of ghost, I realize I probably shouldn't have been thinking about our shared past while our minds were so connected. Could he hear my thoughts over the rush of blood? Or perhaps sense the overwhelming love and affection I feel for him—a practical stranger in his mind?

"Who *are* you?" he breathes, capturing my eyes in his own, searching deep, as if trying to catch a glimpse of my soul. The amazement in his face, the rapture mixed with bewilderment, consumes me and it's all I can do not to break down then and there. To allow the dam to burst and tell him everything, hoping he'll believe me and not run screaming into the night. (Well, to the other side of the cell, in this case.)

But I force myself to hold back, knowing it's not the right time. Not the right place. And instead, I reach out to brush a lock of hair from his eyes with tender fingers.

"I'm just me," I say simply, offering him a small smile. "No one special."

"On the contrary," he says, leaning back down to take another sip. "I think you're quite special indeed. More special," he adds, before sliding his fangs back into my wound, "than I ever could have realized."

12

Rayne

I glance at my watch for what seems the thousandth time as I pace back and forth across my bedroom floor. Mom's already been up here twice to politely (then not-so-politely) ask me to stop the clomping of feet, claiming it sounds like an earthquake downstairs and is drowning out her *Pride and Prejudice* DVD. (As if she doesn't already know the whole thing by heart!)

If only she knew the true reason for my frantic feet. She'd definitely put Colin Firth on pause. Sunny's not back yet. And all the texts I've sent have gone unanswered. I even tried to call, but her phone went straight to voice mail. At first I just figured she had her ringer off, staying in stealth mode. But now, too much time has passed and I'm worried she might be in trouble.

If only they'd invited me to come along. But no, they took off from Club Fang without letting me know, heading straight to Slayer Inc. Manor all by themselves. Sure, I understand why Sunny did it; the girl is always trying to prove she's just as capable as me when it comes to these things. But still! In this case, I could have definitely helped. I'm the slayer. I know Slayer Inc. Manor inside and out. I could have made sure they got what they needed and got back out with ease.

But no. All I get is a text, asking for codes and maps. Which I sent, of course. But maybe I should have taken the initiative to drive out there myself and meet up with them. That way they'd be forced to accept my help.

I glance at my watch again. Something must have happened. There's no way she'd still be wandering the halls unless something went awry. Maybe she typed in the alarm code wrong. Or maybe someone was there after hours, burning the midnight oil, and discovered the intruders. A billion possibilities whirl through my brain on what could have happened to my sister in that house.

I can't take it any longer. I head downstairs and tell Mom I'm running out to the library. Best-case scenario, everything's fine and I've wasted a gallon of gas driving out there. No big deal. At least I'll feel like I'm doing something. And if, by chance, they are in some sort of trouble? Well I'm more than ready to stage a rescue.

I leave the radio off as I drive down the dark, windy New Hampshire roads, heading toward the remote manor. Rain starts to fall and fog laps at my windshield. It's a miracle I don't drive off the road as I navigate the turns with limited vision.

This is just the kind of weather that horror movies are made of, and the feeling of dread creeps into my bones.

Finally, after what seems an eternity, I turn the corner onto the dead-end street where the manor resides. My headlights flash on a dark, abandoned BMW on the side of the road and my heart starts thudding in my chest. I park behind it, then leap out, shining my flashlight at the license plate. Sure enough, it's Magnus's. He and Sunny are still here. This does not bode well.

I leave the cars behind and head into the woods. The fog is as thick as pea soup and the rain pitter-patters onto the leaves above, creating an eerie soundtrack to my journey. I keep my flashlight low, so as not to cause attention to myself, and attempt to navigate over the fallen logs and twisty roots without breaking my ankle.

As I reach the edge of the mansion's side lawn, I slip behind a mammoth oak tree, hoping to stay hidden as I scout out the scene. The old Victorian manor that I used to think looked so cool now looks like a haunted house. As lightning flashes across the sky, followed by booming thunder, I'm beginning to wonder if I should have enlisted some backup for my rescue. Or, at the very least, let someone know where I was going. I try to remind myself that this is just the business office of my employer, a place I've frequented dozens of times. But for some reason the sentiment doesn't make me feel much better.

I ready myself to retreat to the woods, to circle the perimeter until I reach the back of the manor, where I have the best chance to break in without being seen. But before I can make a move, a hand clamps over my mouth.

I try to scream, but the gloved hand allows only a few squeaks to escape from my mouth. I try to bite down but get only a mouthful of thick leather. Strong arms wrap around my waist and drag me, kicking and flailing, back into the woods. I lose my grip on my flashlight and a moment later, I find myself thrown unceremoniously down onto the dirt.

I look up wildly into the darkness, trying to focus on the dark figure hovering above me, silhouetted in the fog. A Slayer Inc. guard? Bertha the Vampire Slayer herself?

No. My eyes widen in recognition. Could it be . . . ?

"You!" Jareth cries. Even in the darkness I can see that his face is full of horrified recognition. "Which one are you?"

"The one you probably don't want to see," I mutter, rising to my feet and brushing the mud off my back. I can't decide if I'm excited to see him or furious that he would manhandle me like that.

"The girl from Club Fang," he concludes. "The one who stepped on my feet."

"To be fair, I was pushed, I'll have you know," I say, deciding to lean toward furious. After all, it's doubtful he's going to be anything but in the way when it comes to my rescue attempt.

"Are you stalking me or something? Didn't I make it clear that I wanted nothing to—"

"Nothing to do with me," I finish grumpily. "Yes, you made it clear as crystal. And no, don't flatter yourself about the stalking thing." I can't believe I ever fell for the guy, the way he used to act. Like he's God's gift to vampires or something. "If you must know, I'm here to rescue my sister. She and your idiot little pal Magnus tried to break into this place to find proof that Slayer Inc. is planning to slay Lucifent. All because a certain vampire general wouldn't take what my sister had to say at face value."

Jareth throws up his hands in disgust. "I knew it." He swears under his breath. "Those fools. They have no idea what they're up against." He paces the clearing like a caged tiger. Which, I have to admit, is kind of hot. Not that I'm thinking about hotness when I'm on a mission to save my sister or anything.

"Well, they went in hours ago and their car is still parked on the side of the road," I inform him. Maybe there is a way we can work together. "Do you think they're still inside?"

"I know they are," Jareth confirms. "At least Magnus. His phone has a tracking device implanted in it," he explains. "When he disappeared from Club Fang earlier, I activated it to track him down. He's definitely in the vicinity."

His words confirm my fears. "This is not good," I mumble. "It's been too long. I'm worried something must have happened to them."

"Well, don't be," Jareth replies curtly. "I'm going to go in and investigate." He reaches into his pocket and pulls out a beige business card with gold script. "Text me in an hour and I'll let you know what I've found."

I raise an eyebrow, glancing at the card, then up at him. "Are you kidding me?" I ask. "I am so not going to go home and wait, if that's what you're implying. She's my sister. And if she's in trouble, I'm going to help her."

Jareth snorts. "You?" he says, his voice full of contempt. "You and what army?"

"I'm an army of one, baby!" I declare, puffing out my chest. Sure, I may not be a vampire anymore. Or even an official slayer. But I'm Rayne McDonald and that makes me kick-ass in and of itself.

"I'm so sure," he replies, his voice rich with derision. "But may I suggest you leave your bravado at the door for a moment? Trust me, I'm the Blood Coven general and I've been around the block more than a few times. There is not a chance in hell a mere mortal would ever be able to successfully break into a highly secured Slayer Inc. administration building."

"Even if the mortal in question had all of the Slayer Inc. security passwords memorized?" I ask, with a slight smile of defiance. "Do you think maybe she'd have a chance in hell then?"

Jareth raises an eyebrow. "And how, may I ask, would someone like you come across something like that?"

"No, you may not. Ask, that is," I shoot back. "You may either admit you need my help or go ahead and botch the whole operation yourself."

Jareth lips pucker with annoyance. I can tell it's going to kill him to acknowledge that I may be even the tiniest bit useful in this endeavor.

"Come on," I urge, dropping my sarcastic tone. "Swallow that pride. It's your friend and fellow coven member's life we're talking about here. You need to suck it up—pardon the pun—and accept all the help you can get, and you know it."

Jareth stubs the toe of his boot against a tree stump, and at first I don't think he's going to answer. Then he sighs. "Very well," he concludes. "You may accompany me if you wish."

"Gee, thanks. So very kind of you to let me tag along."

"Just don't get in the way."

"How about *you* don't get in *my* way?" I know I'm being obstinate. But seriously, the guy needs to be knocked down a peg or ten.

Jareth surprises me with a grudging nod, then turns and starts heading through the woods again, walking so fast I have to sprint to catch up. He expertly skirts the manor's lawn, avoiding any spotlights, until we've reached the back door. He studies it for a moment, taking in the massive lock attached to the remote control panel to the side. Then he turns to me with an expectant look.

"Oh, I'm sorry. Did you need my mere mortal assistance already?" I ask sweetly.

"I don't need it," he clarifies, his voice laced with bitterness. "It just seems unnecessary to go through all the trouble of breaking down a door if you can simply open it with your secret password."

"Now you're thinking," I reply with a grin. "Stand back, vampire, and watch some mortal magic." I approach the control panel, opening the alarm box and pressing the secret code I learned from my Slayer Inc. training. Thank goodness I had been paying attention when Teifert drilled those numbers into my head back in the day. A moment later, the box beeps twice and all three LED lights go green.

I turn to Jareth triumphantly. "Would you care to bust in the door now, m'lord, utilizing your magnificent vampire strength?"

The corner of Jareth's lip twitches. "So there *is* something you can't do."

"Not really. I just wanted to make sure you still felt useful and relevant."

The vampire groans, then reaches out to wrap his hand around the doorknob. The door swings open easily. "All right! Way to go!" I cry in my most encouraging tone, patting him on the back. "Rock on with your bad vampire self, you!"

"Do you mind lowering your voice?" the vampire hisses. "We are trying to be stealthy here, are we not?"

"Oh. Right. Good point." I had been so enjoying teasing him that I almost forgot we're still in dangerous territory and all. "Sorry. Let's do this."

We step through the door and into the dark hallway at the back of the manor. I bite on my lower lip, assessing the scene, trying to remember the best way to get to the stairs, leading to the dungeon below. If Magnus and Sunny were caught, that's probably where they'd be taken. Unless Bertha or another slayer got too eager and—

Jareth's back pocket breaks out into a My Chemical Romance ballad.

"Holy super-stealth, Batman," I note dryly.

The vampire fumbles with the phone. At first I assume to

silence it. But then, to my surprise, he steps back out the door and puts the receiver to his ear.

"Hello?" he whispers as I stare at him in disbelief. "Oh, hey, baby," he says after a pause. "That's so sweet of you. But I'm right in the middle of something now. I can't really talk."

I squeeze my hands into fists. Is he for freaking real? Making mad gestures, I soundlessly urge him to hurry up. He holds up a hand.

"No, no, I'm alone," he assures her as he looks up at me, putting a finger to his lips. It's all I can do to prevent my jaw from dropping to the floor. "Well, I appreciate that. Good-bye, sweetie." He pauses, then laughs. "No, you hang up!" Another pause. "No! You!"

I grab the phone from his hand and throw it across the field. As he watches the phone fly through the air, a look of horror on his face, I shrug. "Sorry," I say. "You seemed to be having some difficulty disconnecting. I thought I'd help you out."

"I can't believe you just—"

"So are we going to do this whole rescue? Or did you need to ask your girlfriend for permission, first?"

Jareth lets out a long sigh, then closes the door behind us, leaving his phone out on the field, where I hope the rain will douse it so it will never work again.

"Fine," he says. "Now where to begin?"

"Oh just shut up and follow me," I growl, no longer feeling excited about our daring rescue. I stalk down the hall, not look-ing back to see if he's following. I can't believe he answered his phone. Not only answered—but was all cutesy to the girl on the other end. That's so not like the Jareth I know. I mean, he's never once talked to *me* on the phone like that!

Jealousy burns at my gut as I push open the door that leads down into the basement, where the dungeon is located. I stare down into the darkness, wishing I still had my flashlight.

"What are you waiting for, all-powerful mortal?" Jareth asks, coming up beside me and whispering in my ear. I jump a mile in surprise.

"Nothing," I retort, trying to still my heart. "Just . . . just looking for a light switch."

"Not a good idea. It might alert someone to our presence." He grabs me by the arm and pulls me close. "Just stick by me," he purrs, his breath tickling my earlobe. "Perhaps I have my uses after all."

13

Sunny

It's been a half hour since the blood transfusion and Magnus is already looking a hundred percent better. The bleeding has gone, the wound has closed up, and his abs are once again the six-pack of perfection they were always meant to be. I have to admit, being a vampire does have some benefits. Namely the amazing power of regeneration.

Which I, on the other hand, am severely lacking. While Magnus did manage to restrain himself from draining me dry, my donation to his health has left me in a very weakened state. Not surprising, I suppose. If I were to have given blood at the Red Cross, I would have at least gotten some orange juice and cookies out of the deal, to help keep me standing. Here I don't even get a dry crust of bread.

I do, however, get Magnus's chest as a pillow, which, let's face it, is better than cookies and OJ any day of the week. I guess he feels bad about my suffering for his sake because after the transfusion, he cares for my wound as best he can in these unsanitary conditions, ripping off a swatch of fabric from his pants and wrapping it around my wrist. Then he pulls me close to him, cuddling me in his nook, arms wrapped around my body, hands softly stroking my back. As I curl up against him, breathing in his warm, familiar scent, I feel a strange sense of peace wash over me. Sure, we're in a bad situation. We may even be in danger of our lives. But here and now, with Magnus gently running a hand through my hair, his fingernails lightly scraping my scalp, I have to admit, I haven't felt this good—this at ease—for a very long time.

I'm not sure of the moment I fall asleep. Or how long I'm out once I do. But at some point I'm awakened by a loud clattering noise outside the cell. I jerk up in bed, peering out into the dimly lit jail. Magnus rouses beside me, looking a little sleepy himself.

"Who's there?" he demands.

"Magnus? Is that you?" a male voice calls out through the darkness.

Magnus is on his feet in a flash. "Jareth?"

Sure enough, a moment later, my sister and Jareth step into view. Seeing us, Rayne turns to her vampire companion, a smug smile on her face. "See? I told you they'd be down here!"

"I never said they wouldn't be," Jareth grumps back. "So save the 'I told you so's' for someone who cares."

Ah, yes. Rayne and Jareth and their infamous bickering. Some things even time travel can't change.

"Sis!" I cry, leaping off the bed with a burst of energy I didn't know I had. "Thank God you've come!" I do my best to hug her through the bars.

"Yeah, well, if you had invited me to begin with . . ."

Oh, here we go. "If I had invited you to begin with, you would be stuck in here with us and thus not available to help us stage our rescue."

She grins. "Touché, sis." As we part from our hug, I catch her gazing at my bandaged wrist with a questioning look on her face. Feeling my face heat, I quickly yank down my sleeve. I don't want her to get the wrong impression.

"Magnus, what were you thinking?" Jareth demands, crossing his arms over his chest. "Coming here alone—without backup. You could have been killed."

"I could have been," Magnus agrees. "But I wasn't. Thanks to my blood mate here." He gives me an affectionate look. "She not only rescued me from a slayer but allowed me to drink her blood to heal my wounds."

Rayne fist-bumps me through the bars. "Score yet another one for us mere mortals!" she crows at Jareth. The vampire general only sighs.

"You do realize that sharing blood with an unlicensed mortal is strictly forbidden," he reminds Magnus.

"It was a matter of life or death," Magnus replies quickly, throwing me a knowing look. "Now are you here to report me or rescue me?"

"Don't be daft. Of course I'm here to rescue you," Jareth retorts, heading over to a nearby desk and rummaging through the drawers, presumably looking for a key. Rayne joins him on the hunt. "I'm just surprised," he continues. "First you run off here on a crazy whim. Then you manage to get yourself captured. And, if that's not bad enough, you decide to drink blood from a practical stranger. I have to say, it's not like you to take such risks."

"Well, we can discuss my risky behavior another time," Magnus declares. "Right now we must get out of here and get to the Blood Coven crypt as fast as possible. Slayer Inc. plans to slay Lucifent tonight. And we must figure out a way to stop them."

Jareth stops his search to look over at Magnus in surprise. "Tonight?" he repeats. "Earlier you said a month from now."

Magnus looks sheepish. "Right. Well, I'm afraid our little . . . intrusion . . . may have forced their hand. Sped things up a little."

"Oh, Sis," Rayne tsks disapprovingly.

"Don't blame us," I declare. "It's Mr. High and Mighty Vampire General who demanded proof. If we just could have met with Lucifent to begin with . . ."

Rayne holds up a key that she's found hanging in a dark nook. "Ta-da!" she cries. "Score another for—"

Jareth yanks the key from her grasp. "Mere mortals, yes,

yes, we get it. God, you're like a pit bull with a bone." He slips the key in the lock and turns. The door creaks open. Magnus and I are free.

"Come on," Magnus says, grabbing me by the arm and hurrying me along. "Let's go save Lucifent."

14

At first I assume Magnus and Jareth plan to take Rayne and me with them as they attempt to stop their Master's murder back at the coven crypt. But it seems they have somehow convinced themselves that we're of no use to them in this fight and they're better off going at it alone. Which is ridiculous, seeing as I saved Magnus's life not hours before and Rayne totally helped Jareth break into Slayer Inc. Manor. But, sadly, they don't seem to recognize our obvious advantages as they take off in their luxury automobiles and leave Rayne and me on the side of the road with our rusty Volkswagen Bug.

But maybe it's for the best. After all, I've got a lot to debrief my sister on. Once we get into the vehicle and close the doors, I turn to her. "We have a problem."

"That Jareth is a huge, pigheaded idiot who refuses to admit the fact that a mere mortal can do anything a vampire can do . . . and probably better?"

"Er, while I'm sure that is very problematic in and of itself, that's not exactly what I was talking about."

"Sorry. Go on."

I draw in a breath, wondering where to begin. "After we fought Bertha, Teifert showed up. And he said something strange. He said there was a good reason that Slayer Inc. wanted Lucifent dead."

"Yeah, we know," Rayne interrupts. "Because he's a child vampire. The same reason Slayer Inc. went after Jareth's family back in the day. It's such a stupid technicality, if you ask me. Who cares if a vampire looks like a little kid forever? What does it hurt anyone else?"

"That's what I said," I reply. "But Teifert looked at me like I had two heads and said they'd never do something like that. Then he hinted there was something else that Lucifent was involved in. Something . . . bad . . . that could hurt the Blood Coven. Not to mention mankind."

My sister furrows her brow. "Like what?"

"I don't know. He didn't elaborate. But, Rayne," I say, a feeling of dread creeping into my bones all over again. "What if we were wrong? What if Slayer Inc. really did have some top-secret reason to take out Lucifent that had nothing to do with his being adult-challenged?"

Rayne bites at her lower lip. "Did we just screw up big-time?"

"Here we are, thinking we're changing history for the better. What if we just made things a lot worse?"

"What should we do?" Rayne asks as she turns the key in the ignition and flips on the headlights. "Should we follow them to the cemetery? Maybe help Slayer Inc. slay Lucifent after all?"

"We could. But if we did, that'd be it. There's no way we'd ever get Magnus and Jareth back after that. We'd be their enemies forever."

"I wish Teifert had been more clear on the details!" Rayne pounds on the steering wheel in frustration. "What if the Lucifent thing isn't a big deal?"

"What if it's a huge deal? What if we've just signed humanity's death warrant?"

"Oh God," my sister moans. She puts the car in gear. "All right, let's go to the cemetery and at least see what's going on. Maybe we can figure something out on the fly."

I nod in agreement—what else can we do?—and a moment later we're speeding down the dark roads, on our way to St. Patrick's Cemetery, home of the Blood Coven crypt. I remember my first trip down into the underground headquarters. The night Lucifent got killed by Bertha. At the time, his murder had seemed so evil. So unnecessary. But now I'm not so sure. What if my murderer was actually a good guy in disguise?

We pull over at the edge of the cemetery, then creep through the dark gravestones toward the crypt. At first I'm positive we're going to end up seeing nothing—that all the vampires will already be deep down inside, where no mortal can enter. But instead, as we grow close, a set of headlights sweeps into view. A long, black limo approaches, pulling over at the entrance to the crypt. A moment later, the door opens and none other than Lucifent himself steps out, into the night air. A little blond boy, dressed in an adorable mini-tuxedo. It's hard to believe someone so tiny and seemingly inconsequential has the power to change the world.

Rayne grabs me and yanks me down behind a gravestone, just as a bellowing cry echoes through the night sky. It's a cry I'd know anywhere.

Bertha.

The slayer leaps over the grave she's been hiding behind, letting out a piercing roar. Without pause, she launches into a round-off back-handspring, flipping toward the Master at breakneck speed, two stakes strapped to her massive thighs. I hold my breath, gripping Rayne's hand in my own. Maybe this is it. Maybe we didn't screw things up after all.

But before she can reach him, Jareth and Magnus step out from the shadows, taking their places in front of their Master. Together they grab Bertha and fling her backward, as if she's a rag doll. The slayer slams into a nearby grave and crashes to the ground.

"Wow," Rayne breathes, squeezing my hand. "I don't know whether to cheer or boo."

Bertha scrambles to her feet, her face twisted in rage. She starts again toward the vampires, her steps slow but determined.

"Halt," Magnus demands. "You are not welcome here, slayer. Walk away now and I will let you live."

"Take another step and you shall dine tonight in hell," Jareth concludes.

"You know people always say that as if it's a bad thing," I

whisper to Rayne. "To be honest, there are some pretty amazing five-star chefs down there. And Bertha, for one, would be pleased to know that calories no longer count."

"Shh," Rayne hisses.

Bertha's mouth lifts in a sneer. "I am a licensed slayer. On an official commission for Slayer Inc., which has been appointed protector of the vampires. If you touch one hair on my head it'll be seen as an act of aggression. And the contract we've held with your kind for centuries will be broken forever." She pauses. "In other words, there will be war."

Rayne and I exchange worried glances. She's right, of course. As much as I'd love to see Bertha dead, I'm not sure murdering her in cold blood while she's on official assignment is the best way to go about it. Especially if it comes at the cost of peace between slayers and vampires. Could this be what Teifert was worried about?

"She's right," Magnus says suddenly, and I let out a breath of relief. He's always been the rational one. "You should go home. We should meet with your leader in the morning. Talk this through. I'm sure we can come up with a diplomatic—"

But his words are cut off as Lucifent lunges at the slayer, so quick I can't follow the movement. He grabs her and slams her against a nearby angel statue. There's a sickening crack as he breaks her neck and she crumples to the ground.

Magnus and Jareth stare at Lucifent in horror. "What have you done, Master?" Magnus whispers.

"Exactly what needed to be done," Lucifent purrs. "Slayer Inc. has been the bane of vampire existence for far too long. It's time to take a stand against our oppressors. And thanks to you two, we now have the perfect opportunity to do so." And with that, he gestures to the slayer's prostrate corpse. "Now come on," he says with a sickening grin. "Dessert is served."

"Oh God," Rayne whispers as Lucifent enthusiastically starts in on his all-you-can-eat Bertha buffet. "What have we done?"

"I think I'm going to be sick," I whisper back, my stomach roiling from the grossness of it all. At least Magnus and Jareth hold back and don't participate in the slayer soufflé. But still. I try to remind myself that Bertha deserves this and more. She killed me, for goodness' sake! But as I watch, disgusted beyond belief, I can't help but hear Teifert's words, echoing through my brain. What have we just set into motion here?

The Master now lives. The Slayer is now dead. We've succeeded in changing history. But to what end? Will there be war between Slayer Inc. and the vampires? And what does Lucifent have up his size six sleeve?

After what seems an eternity, the Blood Coven Master rises from his meal, his mouth and shirt soaked in blood. He frowns, looking out into the darkness.

"Someone's here," he informs Jareth and Magnus. "Bring them to me."

"Uh-oh. I think we've been spotted," I whisper to my sister.

She nods, then rises from our hiding spot. "Hey, guys! It's just us! Nothing to worry about!" I follow her as she steps into the moonlight, a nervous grin on her face. "Just wanted to make sure you were able to take down the big bad. But looks good! Nice work." She walks confidently up to the vampires and pats Lucifent on the head. He scowls.

"Mortals," he cries. "What are you doing here?"

"I've been asking myself the same question all night," Jareth sniffs.

"They're with us," Magnus interjects. He walks over to me and takes me by the arm, then leads me over to the Blood Coven Master. "This is my intended blood mate, m'lord. She was the one who informed me of this plot by Slayer Inc. to end your life. I didn't believe her at first, so I accompanied her to Slayer Inc. Manor to find proof. When we encountered the slayer, I was wounded. If it weren't for this girl, I would have died there in prison."

"And this one helped me break into the dungeon," Jareth adds reluctantly, gesturing to my sister. "Without her, rescue would have been impossible."

"These two girls saved your life tonight," Magnus concludes. "Without them, we never would have been able to take out Bertha."

"I see." Lucifent strokes his chin. "Well, it appears thanks are in order," he says simply. "It is not often that I come across mortals willing to open a vein for my kind."

"No problem," Rayne says gallantly. "Anyone would have done the same."

Lucifent turns to Jareth and Magnus. "And as for you two, you have once again proven yourselves loyal, valuable servants of the Blood Coven. A reward of the highest order shall be bestowed upon you for your bravery and selflessness tonight."

Magnus bows respectfully to his master. "There is no reward greater than the satisfaction of saving your life, m'lord. As you once saved mine."

"You are aware, Magnus, that you would have been made Master in my place, had I perished tonight," Lucifent reminds him. "There could have been much reward in that."

"It is an honor I do not wish for myself," Magnus replies automatically. "I would prefer to spend my days in quiet service, as I have done for the last thousand years."

"You are too valuable for that," Lucifent insists. "I am promoting you to second in command of the Blood Coven. And as for you, General Jareth," the Master continues, "given the current state of things, I believe it would be wise to expedite Project Z. Can you have things ready to go by the end of the week?"

Project Z? I glance over at my sister, who wears my puzzled face. What's Project Z? Could that be what Teifert was hinting about?

Jareth nods. "The queen is completely smitten and has vowed to do whatever I ask of her," he says with a smile. "We are ready for the demonstration anytime you give the word."

"Excellent," Lucifent says, clapping his hands in glee. "What perfect timing, too. The vampire masters are all convening in Vegas for a worldwide symposium and Pyrus shall be in attendance. I shall send word to him tonight, requesting an audience. Once he sees the Blood Coven's display of power, he will be sure to lift our coven to the highest order and we will finally get the respect we deserve. As well as our revenge on Slayer Inc."

O-kay then. This does not sound good. Not good at all. I

notice, out of the corner of my eye, that Magnus also doesn't look too comfortable with the idea. And after a moment, he steps forward. "Master," he says. "What is this Project Z you speak of?"

But Lucifent only grins, patting his protégé on the kneecap. "Come inside, my boy," he says. "We'll open a bottle of Machiavelli and we'll toast this triumphant night. There will be time to talk of such things at a later date. Right now I feel like celebrating."

Magnus bows. "Very well," he says. "But let me say goodbye to my blood mate first."

He turns to me, taking my hand in his and leading me away from the group. "Thank you again for tonight," he whispers once we're out of earshot. "It was definitely . . . interesting."

"Magnus," I say. "I don't like the sound of this. Taking out Slayer Inc.? Impressing Pyrus? Project Z?"

The vampire gives me an indulgent smile. "Don't worry," he says. "Lucifent knows what he's doing. Sometimes he can be rash, but in the end, he is reasonable. He would never do something to hurt the coven, despite what Slayer Inc. might say."

I frown. I wish I could have his confidence in the guy. But after seeing him gleefully slurp down a dead slayer with wild abandon, I'm not exactly feeling the warm and fuzzies for our fearless leader.

"You have done well today," Magnus adds, oblivious to my distress. He brings my hand to his lips and kisses it softly. "I am very much looking forward to the day when I can make you my official blood mate for all eternity."

He pulls me close, wrapping his arms around me and squeezing me tight. I know I should feel warm in his embrace. I should feel safe. But instead, I feel nothing but cold seeping into my bones.

Because no matter how much Magnus trusts his Master, I don't trust him one bit. And I feel like I'm only just beginning to realize the extent of Rayne's and my future-changing mistake.

15

"There is seriously nothing I hate worse than doing nothing." Rayne proclaims, bursting into my room early the next evening and flopping herself down on my bed. She picks at her black-painted fingernails, frustration etched on her face. "I could barely function at school today thinking about everything that happened last night. And when I tried to lose myself in a World of Warcraft raid this afternoon? I ended up getting everyone killed and they booted me from the group."

I give her a regretful smile. "Maybe it's for the best," I point out. "I mean, not about the WoW thing," I add quickly, catching her face. "But as far as doing nothing? We've probably done too much already. I'm thinking it's best we lie low from this point forward. Before we screw up the world any worse than we already have."

"And what? Just sit back and let all hell break loose because of our mistake?"

I sigh. "What else can we do? Go try to slay Lucifent ourselves?"

"I *am* a slayer . . ."

"Not in this world you aren't," I remind her. "And you're not a vampire, either. I just wish we knew what the guy was up to. What this whole Project Z deal is."

"Well, we know it's something designed to impress Pyrus," my sister points out. "And since we know Pyrus is pretty much as evil and power-hungry as vampires come, I'm guessing it's probably not a charitable venture to help feed starving children in Africa."

"Yeah. I think it's probably safe to say he's not planning Operation World Peace," I agree. "But beyond that, we don't have a clue. Besides the fact that it starts with a Z . . ."

"Right." Rayne purses her lips, then pops up from the bed and heads over to my laptop. "Project Z," she muses, loading up the browser. "What could Project Z stand for . . . ?"

"Um, are you trying to Wikipedia a vampire master's secret plan?" I ask skeptically.

"I was thinking more of searching the Scrabble dictionary for Z-words," Rayne replies, scanning the web page. "Like . . . maybe . . . Project Zamboni?" She giggles. "Lucifent's master plan to give the Blood Coven hockey team a fighting chance at the Stanley Cup?"

I snort. "Yeah, that's it. I'm sure."

"Or maybe Project Zirconia?" Rayne adds, using the mouse

to scroll through the word list. "Selling all the diamonds in the Blood Coven vault and replacing them with fakes, all in an effort to solve our current economic crisis."

"Nah. Too magnanimous," I declare. "What about Project Zookeeper? He's figured out a way to cage all the werewolves and create a brand-new tourist attraction to compete with Disney World."

Rayne rolls her eyes and abandons my computer. She wanders over to the bed again, her smile fading from her face. "This sucks," she sulks. "At this rate the world is going to end before I manage to get Jareth back as my boyfriend."

"Oh!" I cry. "That reminds me. What was Jareth talking about when he brought up that whole queen thing? It had something to do with Project Z. He said she was completely smitten and would do anything he asked, remember?"

My sister frowns. "God, that's right. I swear, the guy's got girlfriends coming out the freaking wazoo."

"Or maybe not," I point out. "Maybe it's the same girl you saw at Club Fang. Maybe she's also this queen person."

"Well, I suppose she does look a little inbred," Rayne admits. Then she sighs. "Seriously what does she have that I don't? Besides a tacky wardrobe and piglike eyes?"

"Um, maybe the power to help him launch Project Z?" Seriously, my sister's one-track mind makes her a bit slow at connecting the dots sometimes.

Rayne looks up in surprise. "Oh my God," she breathes. "That explains everything. She's not his true love at all! He's merely using her to help implement his secret plan! Of course!

That's why he never mentioned her when we started dating. She was never really his girlfriend to begin with!"

"Well, we don't know that for sure . . ."

"But don't you see? It makes perfect sense!" Rayne cries, ignoring me, of course. "It explains why he's been acting all goofy and not like himself. It's just an act." She leaps from the bed. "I knew the real Jareth would never play the 'no, you hang up!' game." She turns to me, her face shining with excitement. "This is great. Now all we have to do is stop Project Z and Jareth will be all mine."

I shake my head. My sister and her priorities . . .

"Again, easier said than done," I remind her. "Seeing as we still don't have a clue as to what this Project Z thingie even is."

"Right." Rayne stops bouncing. Then her eyes widen. "Hey, you don't think it could be—"

A knock sounds on the door, causing her to snap her mouth shut. We definitely don't need Mom overhearing us talk about the otherworld. Let's just say, as a fairy princess, she's not exactly a big fan of the undead.

"Sunny, there's a boy here to see you," Mom calls through the door.

My heart skips a beat. I glance over at my sister, eyebrows raised. "Do you think it's . . . ?"

She shrugs. "Well, I don't think it's Jake Wilder . . ."

Mom knocks a second time. "I think he said his name was Magnus or something?"

"Thanks, Mom." I swallow hard. "What should I do?" I hiss at Rayne.

Everything inside me tells me to leap off the bed, burst through the door, race downstairs, and throw myself into his arms. But at what price? Could I end up making things even worse?

"Duh. You should go talk to him," Rayne whispers back. "Maybe you can even get him to tell you what Project Z is. Not to mention get some dirt on this so-called queen."

"Ooh, yeah," I agree, a thrill twisting up my spine at the prospect. "Good idea!" I turn to the door. "I'll be right down, Mom!"

I rush over to the mirror to run a comb through my hair, regretting my choice to not reapply my makeup after gym class this afternoon. At least I changed out of my sweats. Though my ripped jeans and laundry day T-shirt aren't much of a step up, to be honest.

"You look beautiful!" Rayne interrupts, obviously needing a change in her contact lens prescription. "Now go hook up with your boyfriend and try to save the world!"

I don't need a second invitation. I burst out the door, taking the steps two at a time until I reach the front foyer where Magnus is standing with my mom. He's wearing all black, as per usual, with a bright red rose stuck in his lapel. God, he looks so yummy. It's all I can do not to lick him all over.

"Hey," I say, trying to sound as casual as possible. "I didn't know you'd be stopping by."

"I hope it's not a problem," Magnus says gallantly, giving me a small bow. Mom raises an eyebrow.

"Aren't you going to introduce me to your friend, Sunny?" she asks.

I force myself not to make a face. "Um, Mom, this is Magnus. Magnus, Mom." I pray the vampire keeps his fangs concealed until I can get him out the door. And that she doesn't ask too many questions about what classes he's taking this year. Unlike the vampires in *Twilight*, Magnus and the gang learned their algebra and biology the first time around and don't feel the need to repeat the whole high school experience every year for eternity.

Magnus turns to my mother and takes her hand in his, bringing it to his lips for a kiss. "And here I thought you were her sister," he says with a small smile.

Mom turns bright red. "Flattery will get you nowhere, young man," she scolds playfully. "Just have her home before her eleven P.M. It's a school night, you know."

I cringe. I can't believe my mother just lectured a thousand-year-old vampire about my curfew.

"Come on," I say, grabbing Magnus's hand, dragging him out the door and then slamming it in my mother's way-too-curious face. "Parents," I say, by way of explanation, shaking my head. "Can't live with them. Can't shoot them."

"I wish I could live with mine," Magnus replies wistfully, much to my surprise. "But they've been dead a thousand years." He looks a little sad as he opens the BMW door for me. Poor guy. I never thought about him having parents before. He must miss them terribly. Yet another reason I don't understand why people want to become vampires. I can't imagine having all my friends and family start dropping dead while I live on for a lonely ever after. No wonder the guy's so desperate for a blood mate.

I sink down into the soft leather passenger seat as Magnus climbs into the driver's side. He turns up the satellite radio and soft jazz floats from the expensive speakers as we pull away from the curb and start down the road. I'm dying to know where we're going, but at the same time I kind of like the idea of it being a surprise.

We cruise down windy roads and then up a long hill until we reach a secluded wooded circle. Magnus pulls the car to the side of the road. "My favorite spot in the city," he announces, opening the door and exiting the vehicle. He comes around to the passenger side, opening the door for me with much chivalry. My heart beats fast with excitement as I climb out of the car and follow him around to the back. He opens the trunk and pulls out a picnic basket and blanket, making me nearly swoon with anticipation. A vampire picnic in the dark? Could it get any more romantic than that?

He hands me a flashlight, then takes my arm to guide me down a narrow, darkened trail. I wonder, for a brief moment, if I should be frightened. But then I remember, time travel or not, this is Magnus. The most gentlemanly vampire I have ever met. I have nothing to fear from him ever.

The trail widens out to a small clearing at the edge of a steep cliff. I gasp as I look out over the vista; you can see almost the entire town of Oakridge from this height, sparkling below in a sea of multicolored lights. It's gorgeous beyond belief and I've never seen anything like it. It makes our tiny little nothing town appear as magical as a fairy kingdom. Bright stars twinkle above us, dancing around a full moon, completing the scene.

As I stare, breathless, Magnus spreads out the blanket and gestures for me to take a seat. Then he opens the picnic basket and starts laying out a variety of little sandwiches.

"I didn't know what you'd like," he says, sounding a little bashful as he pulls a bottle of blood from the basket and proceeds to pour the contents into a crystal goblet. "And to be honest, it's been so many years since I was able to taste food, I'm not sure what you mortals find appetizing."

"It all looks great," I assure him, rummaging through the sandwiches and searching for something vegetarian. Unfortunately they all appear to have meat, so I grab a turkey and cheese and yank out the turkey, flinging it into the woods when he's not looking, so as not to hurt his feelings. After all, he evidently went through much effort to please me. And I want him to know I appreciate it.

"So," I say, after taking a bite of my rearranged sandwich. "To what do I owe this delicious feast?"

"Must there be a reason for a vampire to take his blood mate out for a meal?" Magnus asks, chuckling softly.

"I suppose not." I grin, taking another bite of bread. I wonder how I can bring up the whole Project Z thing in a casual way. It seems kind of weird to just blurt it out, out of the blue.

But before I can finesse, Magnus speaks. "However, I do admit, there is something I wanted to speak to you about tonight," he says.

I stop chewing, my pulse kicking up a beat. "Oh?"

"As you know, Lucifent has made me second in command of the Blood Coven. And in this position, I am required to accompany him to Las Vegas to meet with Pyrus and the Vampire Consortium," Magnus explains. "And so I was wondering . . ." He pauses for a moment and I notice he's wringing his hands in his lap, as if nervous. "I was wondering if you'd be so kind as to join me on my travels."

I cock my head in question. "Are you asking me to come to Vegas?" This, I was not expecting.

He gives me an apologetic look. "I know it's probably not a trip you wish to take. However, I can't be sure it's safe for you to remain here, all alone." He shrugs. "We broke out of a Slayer Inc. prison, after all. I do not want to leave you unprotected if they were to launch some kind of retaliation for Lucifent killing their slayer."

I stare at him, unable to speak, my mind whirling with the proposition. Should I agree to go with him? Get even more mixed up in this mess than I already am? Then again, what better way to learn more about Project Z if I'm at the scene of the crime?

"So, if I were to go," I say, still not quite willing to commit fully until I talk to Rayne, "when would we leave? I mean, I'd have to pack and tell my mom and all that . . ."

"We're scheduled to leave on the private jet tomorrow evening after dark," Magnus says. He reaches out and takes my hand in his, stroking the back of my palm with cool fingers, causing my heart to go all a-flutter. "It would mean a lot to me if you could come."

I look up, daring to meet his blue eyes with my own. He looks so sincere. So earnest. As if he's already fallen in love with me all over again. The thought makes me happy, yet at the same time, a little nervous. After all, there's so much he doesn't know. So much I'm keeping from him . . .

"There is one other thing," he adds, his voice filled with hesitation.

"What's that?" I ask, wondering what on earth he could be suggesting now. Maybe he's going to tell me about Project Z!

"I don't want you to take this the wrong way," he says after a pause. "But as a mortal, you're very . . . vulnerable. Very . . . breakable, I guess you could say. Even under my protection, it wouldn't take much for Slayer Inc. to take you down, if they decided to go after you. But if I were to . . ." He trails off, swallows hard, then continues. "If I were to turn you early . . ."

I stare at him, my heart literally stopping at his words. "Um, I'm sorry, what?" I manage to spit out. As if I don't know exactly what he's suggesting. As if what he's suggesting isn't the most horrifying thing in the history of suggestions.

He shrugs sheepishly, dropping his eyes to his lap. "You know," he says, "into my blood mate."

"You want to turn me into a vampire," I blurt out before I can stop myself.

"Yes. That is the plan."

"But you want to do it . . . now," I try to clarify. "Like right now? This very second now?"

He nods and it's all I can do not to run screaming into the night. Oh God. This is not good. So not good.

"I think it's the wisest thing to do," he says, steeling his resolve and meeting my eyes again. "And what difference does it make, really? In one month you will undergo the transformation anyway. Why should we wait?"

Um, I can think of about three million reasons . . .

"I don't know about you," he continues. "But I'm not all about the pomp and circumstance like some vampires are. I'd be just as happy to turn you here, tonight, as I would in a lavish ceremony with all our peers. In fact, I think it'd be kind of romantic, sharing something so intimate between the two of us, under the blanket of a thousand stars." He squeezes my hand tightly in his own, his eyes beseeching me. "What do you say, my darling? My Rayne?"

What do I say? What do I freaking say? How about that you don't even know my real name? That you think I'm my sister. That I'm not even supposed to become a vampire at all? My heart pounds in my chest with a hardcore techno beat as I desperately try to figure out what on earth I should tell him. That I'm from another time. That he really doesn't know me at all. That I'm not sure I want to become a vampire—ever—never mind right this second!

And by the way, even if I did someday decide I wanted to become a vampire, I still wouldn't feel right doing it under false pretenses like this. I can't make a lifelong commitment—make that an eternal commitment—to someone I've been lying to all this time. What would happen if he discovered the truth after he'd turned me? God, he might be so angry he'd never talk to me again. And then I'd be alone, for all eternity, trapped in the body of a monster I never wanted to be.

But how can I explain any of this to him? He thinks I've already got my vampire certification. That I've been on waiting lists, signed contracts. He thinks I'm fully dedicated to the process of becoming a creature of the night—and all we're arguing about is a matter of a few weeks. Not life or death!

Bottom line, while I'm a hundred percent sure I want to be with Magnus and I want him to love me as much as I love him, this is a no good, very bad, awful idea.

"I'm—I'm sorry," I say at last, hating the way his face falls at my words. "I don't think this is a good time. I mean, there's so much going on. All this chaos with Slayer Inc. And the launching of Project Z . . . I don't want our moment to be rushed. I don't want to sacrifice the specialness just because we feel pressured by the slayers. They shouldn't be allowed to take that away from us." I give him my most pleading look. "You understand, right?"

He nods slowly, though his eyes betray his total disappointment. My heart pangs at the idea of hurting him, but it can't be helped. "I still want to go to Vegas," I assure him. "I still want to be by your side."

"I know," he says, pulling me into an embrace. "And you're right, of course. There's no need to rush things. I know this is a huge life change and I want it to be as special as possible for you." He pulls away from the hug and gives me a guilty smile. "I guess I'm just excited to make things official. Is that so wrong?"

I let out a sigh of relief. Oh thank God. I've bought myself some more time.

"Good things come to those who wait," I manage to quip, though inside I still feel a little nauseated at my narrow escape. How long can I keep putting him off?

He laughs. "I suppose you're right," he says. "You're always right."

But as he leans in to press his lips softly against mine, I can't help but think of how I feel so very wrong.

16

Rayne

The wind swirls around me, tangling my hair as I make my way down a dark, deserted alleyway, filled with billowing smoke from a nearby exhaust pipe. High above, thick gray clouds succeed in blocking out the sun, giving the landscape a gritty, film noir vibe. The temperature has dropped and I shiver as I press onward, hugging my arms to my chest. I wonder, for a moment, where I am. And where I'm supposed to be going.

Suddenly, a scream pierces the air and I stop in my tracks. A teenage girl with long blond hair whips around the corner, waving her hands frantically in front of her face. Her eyes are wide as saucers and her mouth is twisted in fear. She slams into me, knocking me backward with the force of her fall. As I scramble to regain my balance, she grabs me by the shoulders, shaking me with all her might.

"They're coming!" she cries. "They're almost here!"

I stare back at her, confused as all hell. "Who?" I ask. "Who's coming?"

But she's already released me—pushed past me—sprinting down the alley as if she's being chased by death itself. As I watch her disappear around the corner, my ears suddenly pick up a low groaning sound from not far away. I turn in the direction of the sound, my eyes widening as they fall upon what appears, at first glance, to be a really grungy homeless person, dressed in filthy, tattered rags. But then I get a closer look. At his scarred arms and legs, dripping with greenish pus. At his hollow face, his deadened eyes, his slack jaw. He staggers toward me, arms outstretched, another moan escaping his puffy, blackened lips.

I take a step backward, horrified. I've seen enough episodes of *The Walking Dead* to know exactly what this creature must be.

Project Z. Of course.

I turn to run, but another zombie rounds the corner, cutting off my escape route. A female, from the looks of it, though far from a beauty queen. In fact, for all intents and purposes, she looks like your average seventy-five-year-old grandmother, if your seventy-five-year-old grandmother had a mouth caked with dried blood instead of dried lipstick. From the way her head lolls sideways, I'd guess her neck is broken. Not that this obvious handicap in any way slows her down. As she hobbles toward me on grimy, wrinkled bare feet, I can hear her muttering something that sounds a lot like "brains" under her breath.

My mind races as I try to remember what I used to do to stop the return of the living dead in my Vampires vs. Zombies video game, but unfortunately that usually involved a double-barreled shotgun, and I'm fresh out of those. In fact, I'm fresh out of any weapons at all. I'll have to somehow slip past one of these beasties and pray they're not too fast on their feet.

Zombie number one—let's call him Charlie—takes another jerky step forward, stepping boldly into my three-foot bubble. I suck in a breath and shove him backward as hard as I can, praying he's as unsteady on his feet as he appears to be—and that zombieism really is spread only by saliva, not skin-to-skin contact.

At first I think it's going to work—that Charlie will fall and I'll be able to break free. But the bastard somehow manages to right himself—he's much more agile than the zombies in *Night of the Living Dead*, I must say—and keeps on coming. Behind me, zombie number two—Meredith, we'll call her—gurgles something, then leans over to puke green slime all over my calves. Yum.

Resisting the nearly overwhelming urge to throw up myself, I instead whirl around, extending my vomit-dripping leg to kick Meredith hard in the gut. Luckily, she's not as agile as old Charlie and she flails, falling butt first on the ground, where she writhes in fury. I can't help but think of that old commercial.

Help, I've fallen but I can't get up!

Without hesitation, I make my move, attempting to leap over Meredith and run like hell down the street, praying there are no other zombies nearby. But as I jump, Meredith grabs my leg. Seriously, for a senior citizen whose flesh is literally falling off the bone, she's pretty damn strong, and try as I might I can't free myself from her grasp.

Charlie takes advantage, lunging forward and grabbing me by the neck, then yanking me backward. It's a zombie-on-zombie Rayne tug-of-war as both of them try to bring some piece of my flesh to their drooling mouths. In the end, Charlie is the winner, his rotted teeth chomping down on my shoulder, ripping the skin from my bones.

But just as I start screaming, Charlie's head explodes. Literally. Like brains splattering all over my shirt. His hands slip from my neck and his body goes sliding to the ground. At the same time, I feel Meredith release me as well and realize her head has been separated from her body by an axe.

I look up to find my zombie savior, my jaw dropping when I realize it's none other than Jareth himself. He drops the axe to the ground and grabs me, pulling me into a fierce embrace.

"Oh, Rayne," he cries, covering my brain-splattered face with kisses. "I've missed you so much."

"Um, you have?" I repeat dumbfounded. This is getting weirder and weirder. "Seriously? Since when?" After all, last I heard he hated my guts and wished I'd just go away. It's then that I reach up to touch my shoulder, where the zombie bit me. To my shock and surprise, there's no wound at all.

"Okay, this has *got* to be a dream," I realize, a bit disappointed. I mean, not about the zombie-wound-disappearing part. Believe me, while I love the idea of becoming undead, I prefer the upper-class vampire variety, not the working-class monster.

But when it comes to the part where Jareth is kissing me with wild abandon? That part I really wish were for real.

"Damn. I really need to stop eating all those Fritos before bedtime . . ."

Jareth reaches out and wipes away a smudge of zombie brain from my cheek. "It's not a dream," he tells me. "Well, not exactly."

I cock my head in question. "What do you mean?"

"Think of it more like . . . a vision. Or a warning, maybe. I've been sent here by Hades to have a talk with you."

Uh-oh. I cringe. Here it comes. I'm guessing the Lord of the Underworld isn't so pleased at the mess Sunny and I have managed to make our first few days back.

Jareth leads me over to a small bench that seems to have appeared out of nowhere. He sits me down beside him and finds my eyes with his own beautiful emerald ones. "You were sent here under the assumption that you would help Sunny regain a normal life, as she always wanted," he begins. "But instead, you've managed to put all of mankind in danger."

"Um, yeah," I reply, feeling my face heat at his admonishment. "We're actually still in the process of working all that out . . ."

Jareth gives me a rueful smile. "I'm sure," he says. "Knowing you, you probably have a great big plan in mind. But all Hades can see right now is that things have gone to hell. And not in a good way, either. By allowing Lucifent to live, you've given him the opportunity to introduce Project Z to Pyrus."

I glance down at the dead zombies at my feet. "Let me guess," I say. "Project Z doesn't stand for Zantac and the plan isn't to relieve Pyrus's stomach acid."

"Not exactly." Jareth says dryly, kicking Charlie's corpse with his boot. "And as you can see, even two zombies can cause a ton of damage when let loose. With Lucifent's help, Pyrus will be able to raise an entire army. He'll defeat Slayer Inc. and then move on to take over the world." Jareth's face twists in disgust. "He'll treat humans as glorified cattle, enslaving them and draining them for their blood and then dumping them in mass graves when they're bled dry."

"Which gives Hades's rival, Satan, a bunch of extra souls," I realize aloud. "So he can win their little Hell population competition." So that's why the Lord of the Underworld cares about any of this. He's a competitive bastard, to say the least.

Jareth nods. "You can see the problem here."

I let out a frustrated breath. "God, we were so stupid. We thought we'd try to make things better. And instead we've screwed everything up."

Jareth pats me on the knee. "I'm sure you had the best of intentions," he assures me. "But yeah. You kind of did."

I frown. "Well, it's sort of your fault, too, no offense," I remind him. "You're the one who's setting up the whole Project Z thing to begin with, by hooking up with Tacky Queen of the Zombies."

Now it's Jareth's turn to blush. "You're right," he says, after a pause. "At the time I was so full of hate. All I wanted was re-venge against those who stole my family away. I didn't care what it took—I wanted to destroy Slayer Inc." He squeezes his hands into fists. "But Rayne, you have to believe me—I had no idea of Pyrus's plans to turn against the human race. I trusted him, like everyone did back then. I thought he'd just use the zombies to take out the vampire slayers, then put them back to rest."

"But instead he decides to launch a vampire apocalypse," I say with a sigh.

"He always was a bit of an overachiever."

"So what are we supposed to do?" I ask. "I mean, are we too late to change things?"

Jareth shrugs. "I don't really know," he says. "Project Z was abandoned the first time around, after Slayer Inc. killed Luci-fent. Magnus came to me and told me he didn't feel it was right to take on Slayer Inc., even after what they did to his Master. Especially not with zombies, which could so quickly spiral out of control." He rakes a hand through his hair. "At first I was not pleased by the turn of events. After all, I'd put a lot of work into charming the zombie queen and getting her on our side to make this whole thing happen."

"Yeah, well, she does seem pretty hooked on you," I agree, not able to hide the bitterness in my voice. "It must have been really tough pretending to be infatuated with someone so tacky."

Jareth raises an eyebrow. "Do I detect a note of jealousy in your voice, Miss McDonald?"

I groan. "I know it's stupid," I admit. "But at the same time, I'm pretty much at my wit's end. I've tried everything to win back your love. Instead I've only succeeded in scoring your utter annoyance."

He looks surprised. "Are you saying the past me hasn't succumbed to your Raynie Day charms?"

"That's putting it mildly."

"Well, then the past me is clearly insane," my boyfriend declares. He grabs me and kisses me soundly on the lips. When I open my eyes, we're no longer in the dark alleyway, but in a luxurious hotel suite. Nice. Jareth leads me over to the bed and pulls me close. I relax in his arms, breathing in his warm scent.

"If only this weren't a dream," I moan after a moment, squirming out of his arms. It only reminds me too much of what I left behind. What I'll probably never be able to regain. "I can't even tell you how hard it's been. To see your face, but not your smile. To know that all we shared—all those memories I have of you—don't exist in your mind. And I feel like I'll never get them back."

Jareth reaches out, tracing my now zombie-brain-free cheek with a gentle finger. "I love you, Rayne," he says softly, gazing upon me with adoration. "And I'm sure the past me will someday love you, too." He smiles. "Just keep putting yourself in his path. I'm sure you'll grow on him, just like you grew on me."

"Yeah, like a freaking fungus."

"Oh, Raynie," Jareth says, laughing. "You have to trust me on this. The past me might appear, on the surface, to be a cold, hard barnacle. But remember, I'm just protecting the squishiness inside. The part of me I'm desperately afraid of getting hurt." He smiles down on me. "Get past that wall I've erected like you did the first time around. Show me you're worth trusting. And I promise you, the past me won't be able to help but fall in love with you, all over again."

"I hope you're right," I mutter, crawling back into his arms. I might as well enjoy the dream romance while it lasts. "Because it's hard enough to go around saving the world, without having to worry about saving my boyfriend as well."

"But I'm worth it, right?" Jareth teases, kissing me playfully on the nose. "No matter what the effort?"

I can't help but grin. "I suppose so."

"Rayne, Rayne! Wake up! Wake up!"

I groan in annoyance as rough arms shake me awake. "No!" I cry as I feel the dream slipping away and reality rearing its ugly head. I try desperately to chase the sleep—to find Jareth again for one more kiss. One more caress. One more sweet whisper in my ear.

But it's too late. I'm awake. And my sister's responsible.

"Why did you have to go and do that?" I moan mournfully. "I was having the best dream ever."

"Yeah? Well, I was out living a nightmare," Sunny grumps, plopping down beside me in bed. I glance at the clock. It's only eight thirty. I would have expected her to be out way longer.

"What happened with Magnus?" I ask, rubbing the sleep from my eyes and sitting up in bed. "Didn't things go well?"

"They started out okay," Sunny replies. "I mean, I think he really likes me and all."

"Well, that's good . . ."

"Not really. Not when he still thinks I'm his intended blood mate." Sunny looks at me, eyes wild. "He wanted to turn me into a vampire, Rayne. Like tonight. He's convinced I'm in danger and figures the best way to keep me safe is to turn me immortal." She shakes her head in horror. "It was awful."

Hmm. A devoted vampire boyfriend who wants to turn his true love immortal to save her from harm? I should only be so lucky. "So what did you say?" I ask, already guessing the answer to my question. My sister is nothing if not predictable.

Sunny sighs. "I said no, of course. I mean, what else could I say? But oh, Rayne, you should have seen the look on his face when I turned him down. It nearly killed me, he looked so disappointed."

I groan. God, I wish I had my sister's so-called problems.

"I'm sorry," I begrudgingly tell her. "But Sunny, disappointing a vampire is the least of our worries now."

"Oh?"

"I've learned what Project Z stands for and, well, let's just say it's not ZOMG awesomeness."

My sister leans forward anxiously. "What is it? I tried to ask Magnus, but evidently Pyrus hasn't clued him in yet."

"Probably for good reason." I lean over and whisper in her ear.

"Oh my God," she cries. "What are we going to do?"

"I'm not sure," I say with a shrug. "But I think it's time I pay a little visit to Slayer Inc."

17

can't believe how badly my hands are shaking as I reach up to knock on the front door of Slayer Inc. Manor bright and early the next morning. I mean, what's my problem? This is my future employer we're talking about. The one I'm destined to serve. And this time it's not like I'm here to stage some prison break. I'm applying for a job. A job that, in my time, I already have, so obviously I'm more than qualified to get it.

Yet I can't help but feel a little nervous as I wait for someone to answer my knock. For example, how am I going to explain to Vice President Teifert that I already know my destiny? Last time around he had to corner me onstage in the drama department to break the news that I had a new career path I never wanted. So he's going to be a tad surprised when I beat him to the punch this time. Not to mention when I tell him about the zombies.

I wonder if I should tell him the truth. About the time-travel thing. Would he believe me if I did? Would it help my case? Or would he just decide I'm crazy and slam the door in my face?

Well, it appears I'm about to find out. A hall light switches on and the front door begins to creak open. But it's not Vice President Teifert on the other side.

It's Spider.

I stare at my best friend, unable to believe my eyes. What the hell is she doing here, at Slayer Inc. Manor? Is there some kind of LAN video game party being held that I wasn't told about? (Because that and school are the only times I ever see the girl more than ten feet away from her computer.)

She stares back at me, as if equally surprised at my presence. (I guess I'm a bit far away from the old PC as well, now that I think about it.) "Rayne," she addresses me after a pause. "Um, what's up? What are you doing here?"

"I was about to ask you the same question."

Her gaze darts from left to right and she lowers her voice before answering. "You probably won't believe this," she says, "but I was at school yesterday, minding my own business, when suddenly the drama teacher—Mr. Teifert, I think his name is—pulls me aside. And he says the weirdest thing! You'll never guess."

Oh God. "That once a generation there's born a girl destined to slay all the vampires?"

Her eyes widen. "How did you know that?"

"Long story. Don't ask."

"Well, anyway," Spider continues. "That girl destined to slay the vampires? That's me! *I'm* the destined vampire slayer—just like on Buffy! And here I always thought I was nothing more than a dorky gamer girl who'd probably get stuck sitting on my ass in some lousy help desk job for the rest of my life. But it turns out, that's just my cover. In reality, I'm a freaking vampire slayer. Isn't that the coolest thing you ever heard in your entire life?"

No, it's pretty much the least cool thing, to be perfectly honest. Not to mention the most ridiculous. Spider isn't supposed to be next in line after Bertha to become a vampire slayer. I am.

"I'm afraid there must be some mistake," I say, feeling bad about saying it out loud. After all, she looks so thrilled about the prospect of her new employment. But the sooner she realizes it's all some kind of botched paperwork, the better in the long run.

Her smile fades. "Excuse me?"

"Yeah, as in you're not the chosen slayer. I am."

Now she's frowning. "I don't think so. Mr. Teifert was pretty clear . . ."

"He must have confused me with you," I say, laying a hand on her shoulder, giving her my best sympathetic look. "It happens."

"Since when? It's not like I'm your twin sister! We look nothing alike."

"Maybe not to us, but you know how grown-ups can be. And between you and me, I think Teifert's a bit nearsighted. Not that he'd ever admit it."

"Rayne—"

"It's okay. I'm here, reporting for duty. You're off the hook." I glance at my watch. "In fact, if you head home now, I bet you'll get back in time for some morning PvP with the guild. I know you need your battle points—"

"Rayne, listen to me! I'm not going to just go home and play video games!" Spider retorts, gripping her hands into fists. "There's no mistake. *I'm* the destined slayer. Teifert even told me they injected me with some special nanovirus. If I did go home to play video games, he could activate it. And I'd be killed." She glowers at me. "So yeah. I don't think there's any mistake here. Except the one you're making."

I stare at her. It's all I can do not to have my mouth drop open in disbelief. Could this be true? Could this weird alternate future universe we've created for ourselves really have skipped over me for the slayer gig? I suppose it could happen. Maybe they learned I was the one who broke Sunny and Magnus out of jail? Or that I was present when Bertha was murdered? Maybe they assume, since I've been hanging out with vampires, that I'm no longer the best candidate to serve Slayer Inc.'s interests.

I feel a weird tug of disappointment in my gut. It's funny— back when I was first informed of my slayer destiny, I thought it was a nightmare come true. But now, being left out—being turned down for a job I was supposedly born to do—I feel like breaking out in tears rather than jumping for joy. I guess I hadn't realized how much my role as a slayer had become part of my personal identity.

Do they really think Spider will become as good a slayer as me? Better even? And what if war between vampires and slayers does break out? Will she end up getting slaughtered by brain-hungry zombies?

No. She is innocent. Naive. She has no idea what she's up against, and it's my job to save her from herself. "Spider, look," I try to reason. "I know right now this probably seems kind of cool and all. But trust me, you don't want to do this. It's not all glamorous and fun. In fact, it's really dangerous."

"What, you think I can't handle myself?"

I groan. "You can't even stay alive when we play World of Warcraft. And that's only virtual slaying."

My friend scowls. "Oh, that's nice. Real nice, Rayne."

Sigh. I didn't mean to offend her. "I'm sorry," I say. "I'm just worried about you. That's all. Now is Teifert in there? I need to speak to him. It's very important."

Spider frowns, standing in front of the door. "I'm not supposed to let anyone in . . ."

"I'm not anyone. I'm your best friend," I remind her. I make a move toward the entrance. To my surprise, my so-called best friend leaps into my path, whipping out a stake from her Feed bag. I sigh.

"Really? This is how you want to play it, Spider?" I ask. "Really?"

"I'm sorry, Rayne," she says in a tight voice. "But my orders are very clear. Anyone tries to get into Slayer Manor?" She shrugs. "I'm supposed to stake them through the heart."

18

I stare at Spider in disbelief. Is she freaking kidding me?

"Um, dude. I'm not even a vampire. Why the heck would you go and stake me?" See, this is reason number one why she's completely wrong for the job. She doesn't even get who's stakeable and who should be killed with alternative weapons.

"And how do I know you're not a vampire?" she demands.

"Um, let's see. For one thing, I'm standing out in bright sunlight. I don't have any fangs. I had a garlic tofu scramble for breakfast and I'm wearing a cross necklace," I say, pulling out the necklace in question from under my blouse. A really cool Gothic cross I got on Etsy. "And if you step aside, I can show you how I can walk into Slayer Manor without any sort of invite whatsoever."

"Yeah, but what about that sparkle on your left cheek? Explain that, vampire!"

I roll my eyes. "Hard Candy glitter eye shadow. Which I borrowed from you, if I'm not mistaken." I pause, then add, "And just FYI, if you're really planning to go through with this whole slayer gig? You should know that real vampires don't sparkle."

Her face twists in exasperation. "Fine. So you're not a vampire. But I still have to kill you if you try to come in. Teifert said so and I don't want to get written up my first day on the job." She looks at me pleadingly. "So could you please just walk away or something? Make me look good for my boss?"

"Believe me, I'd like nothing more. But I can't. I have to warn Teifert about a really big threat. It's a matter of life or death."

She shakes her head stubbornly. "No can do, Rayne. I have my orders."

"Fine." I sigh. "Go on, then. Have at me." This ought to be good.

She looks at me, her face twisted in confusion. I look back at her, eyebrows raised.

"Any time now," I encourage her.

She takes a hesitant step forward.

"Hey, isn't that Steve Jobs over there in the woods?" I ask, suddenly turning my head and pointing my finger off into the distance.

Predictably, Spider turns to look. (Because, you know, it's

completely reasonable to expect her dead computer icon to be strolling through the New Hampshire countryside.) I take my advantage, diving past her, up the porch steps, and toward the front door.

My friend shrieks, realizing she's been tricked, and whirls around, reaching out and grabbing me by the back of my shirt, yanking me backward. For a total slayer noob, she's surprisingly fast on her feet. With her other hand, she fumbles for her stake.

I groan. "Really, Spider? I told you, you can't kill me with a stake." Seriously, this is getting so old.

"What makes you think it's a stake?" she demands. Then, to my surprise, she waves the chunk of wood in my direction and flames shoot from its tip.

Holy crap! I leap to the side, narrowly missing getting flambéed by my best friend. "What the hell is that?" I cry. How did she manage to score some magical flamethrower when all I got on day one as a slayer was some stupid stick that I had to carve myself? So unfair.

"Um, Teifert gave it to me. He said I might need it." Spider says proudly. Then she glances over my shoulder, her pride fading into distress. "Um, I didn't know it'd do that, though."

I follow her gaze and realize she's succeeded in setting the porch on fire. Whoops.

Spider pushes past me, trying to fan out the flames. But she only manages to make them rise higher with her waving hands. She shoots me a desperate look. "Um, help?"

I stare at her. "You just tried to fry me like a crème brûlée. And now you want my assistance?"

"Please, Rayne! I don't want Teifert to dock my pay for damages!"

I so want to tell her that working for Slayer Inc. is more of a destiny thing than a paid gig, but I figure there's time to disappoint her later, when there's not a five-alarm fire in the immediate vicinity.

"Fine. I'll help. But you've got to let me in, okay? No more of this trying-to-kill-me thing."

"Okay, okay, whatever," she agrees. "Just get this fire out!" She runs down the porch stairs, then up again, helplessly watching the flames rise higher.

I roll my eyes and walk calmly into the manor. I grab the fire extinguisher I know they store in the closet under the stairs and head back outside.

The fire has gotten bigger at this point, lapping at the roof of the porch. Spider's trapped herself between the fire and the porch rail, just standing there, frozen in place, a horrified look on her face. See? This is why I'm irreplaceable for this job.

I raise the extinguisher and let her rip. A moment later the flames sputter out. Spider collapses onto the porch in tears, choking on the smoke. I walk over and put a comforting arm around her.

"I'm the worst slayer ever," she moans.

"I don't know," I tell her, feeling a surprising sense of pity for my friend. After all, my first day as a slayer didn't go all that well, either. "The firebolt thing was pretty cool. You just need to remember not to use it around flammable materials. Or, you know, best friends."

"Yeah?" She looks over at me with a hopeful look. "You think it was cool?"

"Definitely."

She hangs her head. "I'm sorry I tried to kill you, Rayne. I guess I just got . . . overenthusiastic."

"It's okay. It happens to the best of us." I give her a friendly hug. "Now come on. Let's go talk to Teifert."

19

"Um, Mr. Teifert? There's someone here to see you." Spider squeaks as she peeks her head into the vice president's office. I stand patiently behind her, letting her do her thing. The place is still a bit of a mess, presumably from my sister and Bertha's fight two nights ago, and I wonder how he can manage to work in such disarray.

"I thought I told you I wasn't to be disturbed, Spider," he admonishes, not looking up from his paperwork.

"I know, but . . ." Spider glances back at me helplessly, then turns to her boss once again. "She says it's a matter of life and death."

Mr. Teifert sighs, dropping the paperwork in question onto his messy desk with a totally uncalled-for overly dramatic flair. "Very well. Bring her in."

"Hey, Teif!" I cry, popping into the office and plopping myself down in one of the cozy armchairs across from his desk. "How's it hanging?"

He raises his bushy eyebrows, taking me in. "What are *you* doing here?"

"Well, I *was* here to apply for the whole slayer job—I was told Bertha's no longer in service . . ."

"Yes, thanks to your little friends . . ."

". . . and I was pretty sure I was next in line. Though Spider here tells me she's been offered the gig." I frown. "So what's the dealio, dude? Am I off the list or what?"

"The . . . dealio . . . as you so eloquently put it," Mr. Teifert says stiffly, "is that you decided to break a vampire out of jail and allow him to take out one of our top operatives. Pardon me for saying so, but I assumed your blatant disregard for Slayer Inc.'s best interests meant you were not all that interested in coming to work for us."

"Oh, that." I nod. "Yeah, that was my bad. But you gotta understand, I thought you were only killing Lucifent because he was a child vampire. I had no idea he planned to unleash an army of zombies on the human race." I shrug. "If I had, I promise you, I would have slain him myself when I had the chance."

That got his attention. "I'm sorry?" he says. "What did you just say?"

"Don't play coy with me," I reply. "I know you must know something about Project Z. Otherwise you wouldn't have issued the slay order against Lucifent."

"We knew he was planning something. But we didn't have any concrete details . . ."

"Okay. Well, now you do. It's zombies. Lots and lots of creepy, undead, slimy zombies. Lucifent only wants them to impress his boss. He's a bit shortsighted, that one. But Pyrus is going to take the idea and run with it. Meaning good-bye, Slayer Inc. Good-bye, human race."

Teifert scratches his head. "And how do you know all of this?"

I pause. That is the question, isn't it? But I realize I've got to come clean to someone. And hey, it may as well be someone who might actually, possibly believe me. "Okay, this is going to sound really weird," I tell him. "But I've come back from the future."

He raises an eyebrow. "I see."

From beside me, Spider squeals. "So that's how you knew everything that was going to be in the next game patch! Oh man! I was so wondering . . ." Then she frowns. "And how you knew who was going to win the field hockey game. Dude, that's cheating! I want my five bucks back!"

"Silence," Teifert commands. He turns to me. "So in this future you speak of, we're overrun by zombies?"

"Um, well, not exactly." I give him the shortest version possible (which still ends up being pretty long) about our adventures thus far.

"So I admit, we kind of screwed things up by saving Lucifent," I finish. "But now we want to help make things right. Get him good and dead before he can present Pyrus with his little project."

Vice President Teifert pulls a cigar out of his desk drawer and lights it. Then he takes a puff. I consider reminding him about no-smoking laws in the workplace, but then decide my lungs will have to deal. No need to piss him off when we need his help.

"I'm not saying I believe you," he says at last. "But even if I did, the problem remains the same. Getting Lucifent alone. Thanks to your little Scooby-gang meddling, we've lost the element of surprise. He'll be constantly guarded from here on out." He flicks ash into a nearby empty whiskey glass on his desk. "Not to mention, we're currently one trained slayer short, also thanks to your contribution to our cause."

"No offense, but you didn't want Bertha on the payroll anyway," I point out. "She had a ton of blood pressure problems. Not to mention she ends up betraying you and working for Pyrus in the future. And don't even get me started about her food issues—"

"In any case," Teifert interrupts, "most of our local operatives are occupied with other cases. And while we've started training Spider, and she's doing very well, she's certainly not prepared to go up against any kind of major threat by herself."

"Yeah, she still needs a bit of . . . fine-tuning," I agree with a small chuckle, remembering her performance on the porch.

Spider scowls. "I knew we should have done best two out of three," she mutters.

Teifert taps his desk with his index finger, considering. "I suppose we could call on Riverdale, our sister slayer academy in Europe . . ."

"Oh no!" I cry quickly. "You don't want to do that. They turn out to be evil." Teifert gives me a sharp look. I shrug. "Long story. But we can deal with them later. The zombie apocalypse is a bit more pressing."

"Agreed. But you're not listening, Rayne. We don't have an available slayer to stop them on such short notice. Our hands are tied."

I smile smugly. "But that's where you're wrong. You do have a slayer. You have me. Trained by your very own alternate-future hands. I've staked evil vampires. I've wrestled were-wolves. I've even taken on Tinkerbell." I decide not to bring up the fact that technically I lost that particular battle. Way too embarrassing. "Bottom line, I'm a super-slayer extraordinaire. And with the proper weaponry, I'm sure I could take on a few zombies with one hand tied behind my back."

"You might want to use both hands," Teifert replies dryly. "Considering that with zombies, there are hardly ever only a few."

"Right." I consider this. "Well, maybe the best thing to do is to go after their queen. I mean, if we can't get Lucifent himself, we should try to cut him off at the source. No voodoo queen to raise the zombies from the dead? No zombies for Pyrus to play with. And we all live happily ever after." Not to mention, as an added bonus, I get to get rid of Jareth's little annoying fake girlfriend. A win for everyone.

Teifert stubs out his cigar, only half smoked. "I suppose that would be the best possible tactic, given the current scenario," he muses aloud. "Very well. I will provide you with what you need to go on your quest. On one condition."

I raise an eyebrow. "What's that?"

"You take Spider here with you. She may not be a fully trained slayer, but she has a lot of potential. She could be useful to you in a pinch."

Or, you know, serve as a spy to make sure I'm doing what I say I'm doing. But whatever. I don't mind taking her and her little fire stick along. After all, we've fought many virtual battles over the years. Why not a real-life one?

"It's a deal," I tell him, rising to my feet. "Now let's go check out that arsenal of yours. If I'm going to be facing zombies, I'll be in need of a good old fashioned boom-stick."

20

"Are they here yet?"

I groan, leaning against the abandoned baggage cart, closing my eyes, as Spider asks me the same question she's asked me ten times in the last ten minutes. Seriously, I know she's my best friend and all, but the girl has the attention span of an ADHD-afflicted hummingbird. I can't believe Teifert thinks she'll end up a better slayer than me.

"Do you *see* anyone approaching the plane in front of us?" I ask her.

She looks over at the aircraft in question, still sitting dark on the runway, exactly how it's been sitting since we got here, two hours before.

"Um, no?"

"Well, then I guess they're not here yet, are they?"

She sighs loudly, letting me know exactly how she feels about our intended targets' tardiness, and plops down onto the tarmac, Indian style. I'm suddenly reminded how impatient she used to get during our World of Warcraft raids, always rushing in before the other members were ready. It used to drive her ex-boyfriend crazy.

She looks at her watch. "Don't they know you're supposed to arrive at the airport at least two hours before takeoff?" she sulks. "I mean, hello, post-9/11, anyone?"

"That doesn't count for private planes. They don't have the same security checks," I inform her, trying to keep the annoyance out of my voice. "Not to mention we have no idea when they're supposed to take off. In fact, we're not a hundred percent sure they're even leaving tonight." All I do know is that Magnus told Sunny that Jareth and his little zombie queen were taking the larger of the Blood Coven private jets and would meet them in Vegas.

"Why didn't they just all go together?" Spider asks, peering around the baggage cart to look at the parked aircraft again. "I mean, it seems like a pretty big plane for just the two of them."

Sigh. "I don't know, Spider. I don't—"

"Oh my God!" my friend interrupts, then clamps a hand over her mouth. She turns to me with bulging eyes, pointing furiously in the direction of the airport behind us.

I turn to look, swallowing hard as I realize exactly what's gotten her so freaked out. A parade of what appears to be more than a dozen zombies trudging down the tarmac, toward the plane, led by none other than Jareth and Queenie herself.

"Crap," I whisper, ducking down again. "I thought she'd, like, raise them when she got to Vegas. You know, find a local cemetery . . ." There goes our plan of taking her down before she even boards the plane. We touch a hair on her head and suddenly we've got an entire army of darkness to contend with. And judging from my performance during my zombie dream fight, I can't even manage two, never mind a dozen.

I quickly take a camera phone pic and text it to Sunny. She needs to see what we're dealing with here!

"What are we going to do?" Spider asks, fingering her fire wand anxiously as I send my text. I pray she doesn't make any sudden movements with it, giving us away.

"We've got to get on that plane," I decide. That will buy us some time at least. And then we'll be able to keep an eye on them and see where they go once they land. "Somehow . . ." Though how to actually slip past twelve some-odd zombies, not to mention my boyfriend and his fake girlfriend, I have no idea.

Spider snorts as one of the zombies trips over his own rotting foot and stumbles. "Ew, they're so gross looking," she whispers. "Just like in the movies." She stretches out her arms in imitation and starts walking haphazardly toward me. "Braaaaaains . . ." she groans.

I'm about to tell her she needs to get some brains of her own, when a thought hits me. "Spider, you're a genius!" I tell her.

She stops mid–zombie walk. "I am?"

I reach over and tousle her hair, messing it up. She frowns.

"Um, hello? I just had that blown out, I'll have you know!"

"Trust me." I pull out a case of black eye shadow from my

purse and smear it under her eyes. Then I do the same for myself.

"Oh!" Her eyes widen in sudden understanding. She rips at her shirt, then her pants. "Good idea." Ducking down to the baggage cart, she scoops a handful of grease from the axle and smears it up and down her arms, then covers mine, zombifying ourselves as best we can.

Now I'm not saying we'd score first prize in a zombie walk costume contest or anything, but I have to admit, it's not a bad job, for short notice. And so, as the last of the zombies stumbles past us, we slip to the end of the line, doing our best undead shuffle as we approach the plane, arms outstretched, legs bowed. Seriously, Michael Jackson and his "Thriller" choreographer would be totally proud.

"This is so cool!" Spider whispers as she starts up the stairs in front of me. "Like a real-life video game!"

I shush her and start moaning loudly to keep up the act and drown out anything else she might have to say as we board the plane. As we round the corner into the main cabin, it's all I can do to stop my jaw from hitting the floor.

It's a sight I never thought I'd see. Twelve or so zombies all sitting quietly in their seats, seatbelts securely fastened. Some look eager to get going, while others look ready for an in-flight nap. And is that one in the back actually perusing the Sky Mall catalog?

Flight of the living dead, for realz.

At the very back of the plane stands Queenie, her gaze sweeping over her creatures like a shepherd keeping watch over her flock. Her eyes settle on Spider, who's stopped short in front of me and is currently staring at the scene with an appropriate, yet dangerous level of horror on her face. I shove my friend forward, before Queenie starts getting suspicious, and she quickly picks up the act again, muttering nonsense under her breath as she takes a seat next to a rather dapper old dead guy, dressed in a three-piece suit, accessorized with a crimson cravat. Whatever killed this dude, he definitely died in style.

Now that Spider's found her seat, I scan the plane, looking for a place to sit myself. I realize there's only one spot left. A middle seat between two zombies that look scarily similar to Charlie and Meredith from my dream. Pretty much the last place I want to hang out for the next five hours. But, I realize, as I feel the queen's eyes settle on me, I really have little choice in the matter. And so, swallowing hard, I squeeze past Charlie and plop down into the empty seat, praying that Queenie fed her creatures before the flight. Because I'm guessing the complimentary peanuts aren't going to cut it for this crew.

Once we're all seated, the plane starts its engines and before we know it, we're taxiing down the runway to a point of no return. Once we take to the air, a pretty, blond flight attendant, a vampire by the looks of her, appears at the front of the plane and reminds the undead passengers to remain seated and keep their seatbelts securely fastened until the captain has turned off the sign. As if a little turbulence is going to trouble the corpse in the front row who has already had half his head blown off.

But safety first, I guess.

When the flight attendant's finished, she presses a button and little TVs slide out every three rows and the zombies prepare themselves for the in-flight entertainment movie trailer. And what do you know? They'll be playing *Zombieland*, which is evidently a crowd favorite, judging from the way the audience moans in delight. At least I hope it's delightful moaning. And, you know, not hunger cries.

I try to relax. Close my eyes and go to sleep. But Charlie is laughing way too loudly at every joke in the film—especially when we get to the Bill Murray bit. And Meredith, while keeping mostly to herself, keeps losing her eyeball out of its socket. Which would be gross, in and of itself, but is ten times worse when it drops into my lap and she asks me nicely, through hand gestures and grunts, if I can pop it back in for her.

And just as I'm about to lose my lunch over squishy undead eyeballs, the flight attendant starts wheeling the serving cart down the aisle. And I realize she's not serving peanuts and Pepsi. No, these zombies are getting a full-course meal. Of what appears to be actual brains. And they're chowing down with great gusto.

Horrified, I watch as Spider, three rows up, takes the plate of gray matter that's offered to her with a grim smile affixed to her pale face. She glances back at me, then shrugs and sticks a glob in her mouth. I shudder, realizing I can never speak badly of her slayer skills again. Talk about taking one for the team!

When the attendant reaches my row, I attempt to decline, but Charlie so helpfully grabs a plate and sets it on my tray. I stare down at the squiggly gray matter, which smells overpoweringly like rotten flesh, trying to get up my nerve. But in addition to being a nonzombie, I'm also a vegetarian. And the sight and smell proves too much.

I puke all over my meal, effectively giving my humanity away.

21

Sunny

There was a time when I would have given anything to have Magnus take me out on the town, wine me and dine me, maybe take me to a show, and never once be interrupted by Blood Coven business. To have my boyfriend all to myself—even if it was just for one night. Of course, back in the day that kind of uninterrupted date was nothing more than a sheer fantasy on my part. Even if Magnus did have a so-called free night and agreed to go out, every five minutes the coven would be calling, and he made it clear from the start they were his number one priority.

He was the Master. They were his people. They needed him and he had to be there for them—even if it meant stepping out in the middle of a movie and leaving me alone with my bucket of popcorn. It wasn't fun. It wasn't cool. And there were times,

I have to admit, when his workaholic tendencies almost ended our relationship altogether.

But that, it seems, was the old Magnus. The new Magnus, the one who is supposed to be second in command of the coven, seems pretty content to let his boss do all the heavy lifting. When we first arrived in Vegas, I had assumed we'd head straight to the Consortium headquarters, to find Pyrus and make arrangements to present Project Z. (Giving me an opportunity to figure out a way to stop it all from happening.) Instead, Magnus presents me with reservations to the hottest restaurant in town.

"But don't you have business to take care of?" I ask, staring at the tickets, bewildered.

He smiles. "My first order of business will always be to take care of you," he tells me gallantly. "The rest of it can wait."

It would have been a dream come true, back in the day. But now it's more like a nightmare. Pyrus is ready and waiting. Lucifent's preparing the show. And there's a plane full of zombies landing at Las Vegas airport in only a few hours, from what I've been able to glean from my sister's disturbing text. How the heck can I justify dining out?

"But shouldn't we be helping Lucifent?" I ask. "I'm sure he needs some assistance for his big presentation to Pyrus tomorrow night."

But Magnus only shakes his head. "He told me he and Jareth have it all under control," he assures me, reaching out to squeeze my hand. "We just need to relax and enjoy our time together."

I wonder if he even knows about the zombies. Did Lucifent ever clue him in on Project Z? I'm guessing no—I'm thinking if he did have a clue as to what his boss was really up to, he wouldn't be acting so cavalier. He's Magnus, after all. Protector of the people. The fairest ruler of them all. There's no way he'd be down with letting loose an army of the dead on Slayer Inc., never mind the general population.

Unfortunately every time I try to bring it up, he cuts me off, telling me he doesn't want to talk business tonight. He doesn't want to think about vampires or the Consortium or any kind of projects—from A to Z. Tonight he wants to spend time with a pretty girl and enjoy all of what Vegas has to offer.

So I do my best to enjoy myself. Try to remind myself that this is exactly what I wanted. But in the end I find I can barely hold a conversation. And by the time we get back to our hotel room at the Wynn, I can tell Magnus thinks something's wrong.

We stand outside the room and he pulls out a key card, handing it to me and inviting me to open the door. From the anxious look on his face, I get the feeling there's something special inside and my heart starts fluttering as I slip the card into the reader and step into the room, wondering what on earth it could be.

The first thing I notice is all the candles, placed on every available surface and giving the room a warm, golden glow and sweet scent. Then my eyes find and follow the trail of dusty pink rose petals winding toward the king-size bed. On the white cloth–covered bedside table is a bottle of champagne—

Cristal—chilling on ice, alongside two silver flutes. It's a scene of seduction right out of a Hollywood film. But I'm guessing it's not sex Magnus has in mind. At least not only sex . . .

As I stare at the room, too shocked to move, the vampire steps in beside me, snaking a hand around my waist. My body lurches at his unexpected touch. "Do you like it?" he whispers in my ear.

Do I like it? Once upon a time I would have thought I'd died and gone to Heaven to see such a love nest, created by my busy boyfriend. Back then he was too preoccupied to ever do something so romantic. Now, I realize, because of Rayne's and my actions, he has nothing better to do than to spend his existence trying to make me smile.

And I should be smiling. I should be thrilled. Instead, I'm filled only with dread.

"Wow," I say, forcing my feet to step farther into the room, escaping his tender touch. "It's really beautiful. And so . . . unexpected."

He comes up behind me, wrapping his arms around my waist again, dragging me close to him and nestling his head against my back. "I wanted to surprise you," he says, stroking my stomach with gentle fingers, sending my pulse skittering like a frightened cat. "I wanted to make sure tonight was special for you."

"It's . . . very special," I stammer, inhaling sharply. Can he hear my heart hammering in my chest? I'm almost positive it's drowning out the soft jazz, drifting from hidden speakers.

He brushes away my hair and presses his lips to the nape of my neck. I shiver at the slight scrape of fangs against my delicate skin. "All I want to do is make you happy," he murmurs. "For the rest of your immortal life. Which," he adds, pulling me around to face him, taking my hands in his own, "will start tonight."

I leap back, startled out of my trance. He furrows his brow at my reaction. "What's wrong?"

"Look, Magnus," I say, trying to keep my composure. "I thought we agreed we were going to wait."

His smile falters, a shadow crossing his face. "Only so I could make it special for you," he reminds me. He gestures to the romantic room. "Which, as you can see, I have tried my best to do . . ."

Oh God. This is not good. My heart is now pounding in my chest with the force of a sledgehammer and I don't know what to do. I've run out of excuses and evidently out of time. If I say no now, he's going to be angry. I'm going to lose my in and my only chance to stop Lucifent. But if I say yes, I realize, the consequences are going to be far worse.

"Magnus, I don't know," I try to hedge. "I mean, there's so much going on right now. Shouldn't we be concentrating on Lucifent's presentation to Pyrus?"

Magnus's eyes narrow. He drops my hands and walks over to the bed. With an angry gesture, he sweeps the rose petals from the comforter and sits down.

"You seem awfully concerned about Lucifent," he says

sourly. "In fact, you haven't stopped talking about him since we got here." He looks up, his eyes rimmed with red. "Is there something you're not telling me?"

I sit down beside him on the bed, reaching over to take his hand in mine. "I'm sorry," I say. "It's just that I can't help thinking about the battle between Slayer Inc. and the Consortium."

He squeezes my hand, his face softening. "Sweetheart," he says, "you need to stop worrying about that. Lucifent has everything under control." He pulls my hand to his lips and starts kissing the back of my wrist.

I pull my arm away. "Yeah, I know. That's the problem."

Magnus cocks his head in question. "What do you mean?"

"I mean, do you really think it's a good idea to take out Slayer Inc.?" I ask, searching his face for answers. "After all, they've been policing vampires for centuries. Keeping all the checks and balances. To remove that removes all the security measures that have been put in place. And then there's nothing to stop, say, an evil dictator who wants to destroy the human race." I take in a breath, daring to continue. "Look, Magnus, I know Pyrus is your head honcho and all. But have you taken a close look at his politics? Do you really think he's the leader that the Consortium needs to take the vampires through the millennium?"

Magnus grits his teeth. "Rayne, you're new to all of this. And I appreciate the fact that you're interested in the politics. But dearest, you don't know what you're talking about when it comes to Pyrus."

"I know more than you. You don't even know what Project Z is!" I blurt out before I can stop myself. But I need him to take me seriously.

He lifts an eyebrow. "And I suppose you do."

"Yes. Actually I know a lot of things," I say. "And you need to listen to me. If you don't get involved with what's going down, there are going to be huge consequences."

Magnus rises from the bed, stepping over to the window. He stares out onto the Vegas strip, shimmering and shining in its multicolored brilliance. I wonder, wildly, when vampires rule the world and zombies roam the streets, if they'll bother to keep the lights on.

"You need to be careful what you say," he says at last, still staring into the night. "Especially about Pyrus. It could be seen as treasonous if someone were to hear you. They could revoke your membership, meaning we could never be joined . . ." He trails off, then turns to face me, his eyes drilling into my soul. "But maybe that's your plan," he realizes aloud. "Maybe that's why you've been so hesitant about joining me. You're only here as a spy. Drawing me in, making me care about you, allowing you into my world . . ."

My heart breaks at the hurt in his voice. "Magnus . . ."

"That's it, isn't it?" he demands. "You're a spy. For Slayer Inc. or someone else. You never wanted to be with me. This is all just subterfuge."

"It's not like that," I reply flatly. "You don't understand."

"Then make me!" he cries, his voice anguished. "Make me

understand why you're so hot and cold. Why you melt against me one moment, then pull away the next." He rushes to me, grabbing my hands, a desperate look in his eyes. "Please," he begs, dropping to his knees. "What aren't you telling me?"

And so I tell him. Everything. About the time travel. Our previous relationship. What Rayne and I have been trying to do this time around. As I speak, his hands clench mine so tightly, I wonder if he'll break my bones. But I can't stop the truth spilling from my lips.

"Project Z stands for *zombies*," I finish at last. "And if Lucifent is allowed to present them to Pyrus, we may as well kiss the human race good-bye."

Magnus rises to his feet, staring down at me as if I'm insane. "Time travel?" he repeats. "Zombies? You are seriously out of your mind."

"But I'm telling the truth!" I insist, wishing so badly I had started telling the truth from the start. Then maybe, just maybe, I wouldn't be in this mess. "The zombies are on their way. We don't have any time to waste. We have to stop Lucifent from presenting them to Pyrus . . . by any means necessary."

Magnus stops in his tracks. "What are you saying?" he demands in a cold voice. "You want me to kill my own sire?"

I draw in a breath, forcing the hysteria from my voice, knowing it'll only hurt my case. "Yes," I say slowly. "If he won't listen to reason."

"Then you're as bad as Slayer Inc."

"But Slayer Inc. was right!" I protest, feeling like I'm losing the battle. What can I say to make him believe me? "I didn't know it at the time—I thought he was innocent, just like you. But now I see he's not. And he must be stopped. The fate of the world depends on it, don't you see?"

"All I see is a liar and an enemy to the coven," the vampire growls. "A snake who has slithered into our midst in a pathetic attempt to destroy us from the inside out." He glares at me with hatred in his eyes. "You know nothing about Lucifent or Pyrus or any of the other vampires. And if you think I would ever believe your wild tales—well, you know nothing about me either!" He grabs the bottle of champagne and throws it against the wall. It shatters into a thousand pieces, alcohol spraying everywhere.

"Magnus!" I beg, tears gushing down my cheeks. "Please. Just listen to me! I swear I'm telling the truth! Just ask them! Just ask them about Project Z!"

But he's already on his phone, calling the guards to take me away.

22

Rayne

The gig, as they say, is up. I've got puke on my shirt and a plane full of zombies staring at me with eager eyes. And one zombie queen, storming up the aisle in my direction. My only weapon—a semiautomatic pistol, stashed under my seat, isn't going to be all that useful in a crowd, even if I did manage to avoid shooing out a window and depressurizing the cabin.

It doesn't take long for Queenie to reach me. "You!" she cries. "You're not one of my children." She stares at me, as I try to come to terms with the fact that she considers these corpses family. That may explain a lot. "Why . . . you're . . ." Horrified recognition washes over her face. "The girl from the club!" She looks over at Jareth, who is now also standing above me, peering down with a surprised look on his face. "What is the meaning of this?" she demands.

Jareth ignores her, choosing to address me instead. "Well, well, if it isn't the mere mortal," he says. "You really can get in everywhere, can't you?" Hmm. Do I actually hear a thread of admiration in his voice?

"What is she doing here?" Queenie screeches, with no admiration whatsoever.

He chuckles softly. "I can promise you, dearest, as always I haven't the slightest clue as to Miss McDonald's motivations."

I stifle a chuckle. Queenie stares down at me with venom in her eyes. She opens her mouth to speak but is cut off by a sudden squeal two rows up. "Ew!" Spider cries, leaping from her seat. "Watch the drool, dude!" She wipes her arm on the seat cushion, a grossed-out look on her face. Great. I guess we're both busted now.

Queenie marches up to Spider, grabbing her roughly by the arm and dragging her back to Jareth. The vampire gives her a critical once-over. "There's another one of you?" he asks derisively. "I guess at least this one's not a triplet."

"See?" Spider mutters. "I told you we look nothing alike."

"Look, can we talk to you?" I ask Jareth, figuring we might as well come clean. Well, as clean as possible with puke running down my shirt and Spider's arm caked in zombie goop. I glance over at Queenie. "Alone?"

"You know, anything you have to say to my boyfriend—" Queenie starts. Jeez. She really is like in third grade, isn't she? Luckily Jareth cuts her off.

"It's okay, darling," he assures her, reaching out to kiss her on her cheek. How much effort must he be making to be so sweet to someone so nasty? "You stay here and take care of the children," he says. "I'll take care of our little stowaways in the back."

Queenie reluctantly agrees, though she doesn't look like she likes it. As she walks down the aisle, we follow Jareth to the back of the plane, through an ornate-looking wooden door and into a second cabin. Unlike the standard setup of the front cabin, back here is a luxurious sitting area, draped in crimson and black with a bar stocked with bottles of blood. Totally Air Vampire chic.

Spider surveys the scene, letting out a low whistle. "Toto, I don't think we're flying Southwest anymore."

Jareth closes the door behind us, then turns, his face expectant. "So," he says in a smooth voice. "To what do I owe this dubious honor?"

"Um, the crap tables were calling and we hate flying coach?" Spider, to her credit, tries. But Jareth just rolls his eyes at her, then turns to me.

I snort. "No offense, dude, but you're the one with the plane full of zombies," I remind him. "Maybe you're the one who needs to start explaining."

"That is none of your business."

"Actually," I correct him. "It kind of is. I mean, have you ever seen *Night of the Living Dead*? It's one of the few horror flicks where not even a virgin, sober white chick survives at the end."

"So, what? You think twelve zombies will bring about the apocalypse?"

"Twelve zombies, no. But once Pyrus gets his hands on Queenie out there, he's going to raise a few more. Like an entire army's worth. Meaning we can pretty much kiss that whole happily-ever-after-for-the-human-race fantasy good-bye."

"I don't know what you've heard," Jareth replies. "But I can assure you, this has nothing to do with your precious human race. We are only using them to go after Slayer Inc. And they more than deserve what's coming to them."

"Slayer Inc.?" Spider cuts in, in an indignant voice. *Uh-oh.* "What did Slayer Inc. ever do to you?"

Jareth whirls around to face her, his eyes practically bulging from his head. Oh dear.

"Excuse me?" he demands in a tight voice.

Spider lets out a small *eep* and backs away quickly. "Um, I mean, just for conversation's sake," she stammers. "Not like I like them or, you know, work for them or anything."

"Actually Jareth's got a pretty decent reason to hate Slayer Inc.," I butt in quickly, before she can make herself sound even more suspicious. "At least the old Slayer Inc. They killed his family, back in the day. Because his brother and sister were child vampires."

Jareth thankfully abandons Spider, turning his attention back to me. "How do you know that?" he demands, his eyes filled with suspicion. "How do you know about my family?"

"It doesn't matter. The point is, that was the old Slayer Inc. Today's organization would never do something like that."

"But they did." The vampire crosses his arms over his chest. "Two nights ago. Remember? They sent Bertha after Lucifent because he was a child vampire. In fact, you and your sister were the ones to warn us in the first place."

Sigh. "Yeah," I admit. "Our bad. Turns out they actually had a really good reason to take him out."

"Which was . . . ?"

"Um, the whole unleashing-an-army-of-zombies-on-the-world thing?" I remind, gesturing to the front cabin. "You gotta admit, that's pretty harsh."

"Once again, I can assure you—"

"—you're just after Slayer Inc. So you say. But how do you really know?"

"How do *you* really know? You were obviously wrong before."

I knew he was going to say that. And what am I supposed to tell him? That the future him came to me in a dream and warned me about Pyrus's real intentions? He's so not going to buy that.

"Dude, I totally get that you're out for vengeance and all," I say, trying a different tack. "But from personal experience, let me tell you, that whole eye-for-an-eye thing never really works out in real life. And you have to admit, the Slayer Inc. of today provides a valuable otherworld police force. They keep the peace. They protect both humans and vampires from those who want to do them harm. Imagine a world without them. It would be chaos. No checks and balances. No laws. Any evil dictator could just swoop in at a moment's notice and wreak havoc on the world." I shrug. "Bottom line, Lucifent is still alive and no worse for wear. Isn't it best to make peace and move on?"

"I will never make peace with Slayer Inc." Jareth declares vehemently. "You weren't there. You didn't see my sister's face when that slayer stabbed her through the heart."

Maybe not, I want to say. *But I did see your sister and the rest of your family living happily ever after in an awesome castle down in Hades, loving their afterlife.*

If only there were a way I could let Jareth see his sister's smile. Let him hear his mother's laugh. Smell his dad's barbecue. I feel like only then—knowing how happy and safe they are, and knowing how much they want him to feel happy and safe, too—only then will he be able to let go of the hatred, anger, and guilt he's been harboring for so many years.

I turn to Spider. "Do you mind if I talk to Jareth alone for a second?" I ask.

She looks hesitant. "You don't want me to go . . . out there . . . again, do you?" she asks warily, pointing to the zombie cabin with a shaky finger.

Good point. I scan the room. "How about the bathroom? We won't be long, I swear."

Thankfully she nods. "Good idea. Then I can wash off some of this nasty zombie goop." She skips over to the bathroom, ducking inside and closing the door behind her. Once she's gone, Jareth turns to me.

"So tell me," he says in a tight voice. "Who are you really and where did you come from? And don't pull any more of this mere-mortal crap with me. I know there's something you're not telling me, and I want to know what it is."

"You're right," I reply, drawing in a breath. Here goes nothing. "I'm Rayne McDonald. And I'm from the future."

"Right." He snorts. "That's a good one."

"It's good because it's true," I insist. "Think about it for a second. How else would I know all the things I know? About your family. About you."

"And what, pray tell, do you know about me?"

There's so much. Where can I even begin? "I know you used to be a sculptor," I start. "And that you can still see much of your work around Europe. I know you loved your art but gave it up after your family died—too painful of a reminder of what you'd lost. I know that after their deaths you vowed to walk the earth alone and swore never to love again." I pause, then add, "And I know that you will change your mind. That you will fall in love. That you'll fall in love with me."

Jareth frowns. "Impossible!"

"Is it?" I cry. "Is it so hard to think of a future where you're not full of hate and rage and revenge? Where you've been able to let go of your deepest fears and most painful memories and dared to trust another person besides yourself?"

"You're making this up," Jareth insists angrily. "And you've told me nothing that you couldn't have found out on your own. If you're really from the future—if I've really shared all this so-called pain with you—then tell me my deepest secret. The one I've never told anyone before."

I nod slowly, wishing I didn't have to do this. He may be asking for it, but he doesn't really want to hear it.

"You think it's your fault your sister was slain," I say at last. "Because you ran away instead of helping her."

Jareth's face turns white as a ghost. He doesn't speak. He doesn't move. He just stares at me with eyes clouded with confusion and fear. I hold my breath, praying I haven't made a wrong step. That he won't erupt in rage and kill me on the spot for saying the words aloud. But I had to get him to believe me. Otherwise none of this will matter.

Finally, after what seems an eternity, he opens his mouth to speak. "I've never told anyone that," he says in a quiet voice.

"Not yet you haven't," I correct kindly. "But you will. Because you trust me. And you know I'm worthy of your trust."

He closes his eyes, his face a war of emotions. I wait patiently for him to digest all I've said. I know it's a lot to take in. Too much, perhaps. But the clock is ticking. And I have to convince him I'm worth trusting in other matters as well, before we land and it's all too late.

"Your future self trusts me with your most painful secrets," I say gently. "All I'm asking is that you trust me in this as well. Project Z is not what you think. Pyrus will take the zombies Lucifent offers him and wipe out Slayer Inc., yes. But he won't stop there. He'll raise more zombies—an army's worth—and start a war with humanity, relegating humans to nothing more than cattle to be milked for their blood. Vampires will revert back to the monsters they once were. No longer civilized, no longer bettering the world, but destroying it instead. And there will be no one to stop them." I give him a rueful look. "I know why you hate Slayer Inc. But we need them now. Or everything you've worked so hard for over the years will be destroyed."

Jareth paces the room like a caged tiger, raking a hand through his tousled hair. "This is impossible," he mutters under his breath. "It's got to be a trick somehow."

My shoulders slump. Defeated. He's so stubborn—just like me. And unless I can get him to believe me about the time-travel part, he'll never believe me about the rest. But how can I prove it to him? How can I show him all I've seen? Back when we were blood mates, we had a connection. I could call on him, push messages into his brain. But now . . .

That's it. My mind races with the idea. Could it actually work?

I have to try. We're almost out of time.

"I can prove it!" I blurt out before I can lose my nerve. "I can prove everything I've been saying."

He spins on his heel, looking down at me, the tiniest shred of hope written on his face. He wants to believe, I realize. Badly. "And how can you do that?" he asks in a voice filled with hesitation.

I hold out my wrist. "Bite me."

"What?"

"You want to know the truth? Then take it from me. See what I've seen. Hear what I've heard. Only then will you be convinced that I'm telling you the truth."

Jareth shakes his head. "No," he says. "It's against the rules. It's against everything I've vowed to uphold."

"I can show you your sister," I say quietly.

His eyes narrow. "How could you possibly—?"

"Wouldn't you prefer to see for yourself?"

He squeezes his eyes shut, then opens them again. "If you're lying . . ."

"If I'm lying, you can drain me dry. Kill me here and now and be done with me forever. How about that?"

He sighs.

"Come on, Jareth. Will you really be able to live your life, knowing you had a chance to see your sister one last time, but you walked away?"

"No," he says resignedly. "I suppose not."

And so, he takes my wrist in trembling hands and brings it slowly to his mouth. As I hold my breath in anticipation, I feel his fangs slide into my veins. I wait for the ecstasy I know should be coming. The feeling of connection between two people sharing one blood. But instead of the joy, all I feel is a chilling fear and overwhelming suspicion.

He doesn't believe. He's closed his mind. And I'm going to have to work as hard as hell to make sure he sees what he needs to see before he pulls away.

And so I close my eyes and push, with all my mental might, bringing him back to the morning in Hades when we walked up to his family's castle. When his sister came bursting from the front door, throwing her arms around him with wild abandon. When she told him the truth about what really happened to her. How her death was not his fault after all.

"Jareth, I can bend people's wills," she explains. "It's some-

thing I've been able to do ever since I first turned into a vampire." She shrugs sheepishly. "That night, well, I knew you'd go
in there, fangs blazing, trying to take them all out yourself—
even if it meant your own death. So I placed a hold on you. I
suggested you stay in one place. I mean, you had all those other
vampires in the Blood Coven to worry about. I couldn't rightly
let you sacrifice yourself for me."

Jareth stares at her, shaking his head in disbelief. "So I didn't
leave you?"

"Not of your own free will, anyway. There was no way on
earth you could have resisted the power of my suggestion," she
assures him. She reaches out for her brother's hands again, finding his eyes with her own cool blue ones. "Jareth, you didn't
cause my death. I saved your life."

Jareth smiles against my wrist, and I can feel bloody tears
splash on my skin. My own eyes water as I realize how much
this means to him. How close I feel to him now, linked as one,
sharing his overwhelming relief and joy to finally know the
truth. I'd love to let him stay here in this memory forever. To
give him time with his sister and family, soaking in all the love
he's missed all these years. But we have to move on. We have
darker places to go before this is all said and done.

And so I show him the rest. Pyrus. What he's capable of.
How he plans to turn their democracy into a dictatorship. What
he really plans to do with Project Z.

But we have the power to stop him, I remind Jareth. Stop
him now before any of this comes to pass.

And then, at last, I show him us. I know it's probably not

the most on-target stuff I should be focusing on. But how can I waste my one opportunity to share with him the memories I have of our love? I free my mind and let the images flow, letting him experience all we've shared together. I end with that night in Hades, when I was forced to leave him. And the promise I made to find him here and make him love me all over again.

At last, Jareth pulls away, his fangs sliding easily from my wrist. He takes a white bandage and ties it carefully around me, stopping the blood from flowing too fast. Then he looks up at me, blood tears streaming down his cheeks. I reach out, squeezing his icy hand in my own, trying to warm it with my fingers.

"I never thought I'd see her again," he whispers, dropping his gaze to my hand. "And what she said . . ." He trails off, then looks up again, his face awash with appreciation and awe. "I can't even tell you what you've just given me," he murmurs. "I will never be able to repay you for that gift . . . as long as I live."

"Yes, you can," I assure him, forcing my voice to be strong. "By helping us defeat Pyrus before he gets too powerful. We still have a chance if we work together."

He nods resolutely. "Of course," he says. "The last thing I want is to start a war that will kill more innocent people. Just like my family was killed." He swallows hard. "We have to put an end to this. Now."

"Well, we can start by calling off the zombies. Letting Queenie out there know you've changed your mind. That you no longer need her services. Tell her to send the zombies back to their graves where they belong before they do any harm."

Jareth agrees, then chuckles softly.

"What?" I ask, feeling my face heat, but not sure why.

"You thought she was my girlfriend," he says. "For real."

"Yeah," I admit. Now my face is burning red. "Though I was surprised, to be honest. She didn't seem like your type."

"And what is my type, may I ask?" Jareth asks in a teasing voice. And suddenly I realize his face is very close to mine.

I grin. "A mere mortal who won't take no for an answer?"

He laughs, a sweet gentle laugh. The kind of laugh I've missed hearing for so long. Then without warning, he pulls me close. So close I can feel his breath on my lips. Oh God. Is he really going to do it? Am I really going to experience our first kiss . . . all over again?

But just as his lips brush my skin, a screech echoes through the chamber. We break apart, whirling around to see what on earth could have made such a horrific noise.

It's Queenie, standing in the doorway, her face twisted with fury as she stares down at us. "How dare you?" she demands in a cracking voice. "How dare you betray me?"

Jareth's eyes widen in fear. "Look," he tries. "Glenda! I can explain!"

But Queenie—Glenda—doesn't seem interested in any explanation. She's already turned to the intercom attached to the wall next to the door. She pulls the transmitter to her mouth, still glaring at Jareth with utter disgust.

"Attention, passengers," she purrs into the mic. "The captain has turned off the seatbelt sign. You are now free to *eat* around the cabin."

Uh-oh.

23

Sunny

It doesn't take long for Pyrus's guards to show up. Magnus refuses to meet my eyes as they handcuff me and gag me and drag me away. I can't tell you how much it hurts to know he turned me in like that, but I suppose I shouldn't be shocked, knowing his character like I do. It's funny, I've always admired his sense of unwavering loyalty, even though this isn't the first time it's been completely misguided. To trust so completely that what you believe in is right and true—it's something I've never been able to do myself. I'm always searching for ulterior motives or double-crossing. Which is one of the reasons he and I had our problems the first time around.

But now the tables are turned and he's the one who doesn't trust me. And for good reason, I suppose. I lied to him. I pretended to be someone I wasn't. I led him to believe I wanted to become a vampire. No, not only a vampire, but his blood mate for eternity. The girl he'd been waiting to arrive for a thousand years.

And all the while I conspired against his bosses. The vampires he's associated with for centuries. Of course he'd trust them over me. In his mind he just met me a few days ago. And I've done nothing but deceive him since.

Still, all the rationalization doesn't dull the ache in my heart as I realize I've probably lost him forever. Any chance we had for a happily-ever-after in this new reality is gone for good.

Oh and the ever-after part? Turns out that might be shorter than expected as well.

After leaving me in some kind of holding cell for about an hour, the guards finally return, handcuffing me again and leading me into a private elevator, which shoots us fifty stories up. We emerge in a luxurious penthouse—as fancy as they get—with floor-to-ceiling windows overlooking the brightly lit Vegas strip. The place makes the suite in *The Hangover* look like a Motel 6 and is almost as badly trashed. Pyrus evidently likes partying hard in the city of sin.

Because, yes, we're in the House Speaker's suite, where I spot the man in question lounging on a fancy sofa, dressed in a silk gold-and-black dressing gown and sipping blood from a martini glass. Across from him sits Lucifent, who looks ridiculous in this lavish adultlike setting. A little boy, legs too short to even reach the floor, dressed in a tuxedo and downing shots of blood. It's surreal, to say the least.

"Pyrus, have you seen the bottle of Louis the Sixteenth we'd opened to let breathe?" asks a voice to my left. I whirl around to see none other than Magnus walk into the room, holding a pair of wineglasses in his hands. He's dressed more casually than the other two, in a pair of slouchy black jeans and a tight black T-shirt that accentuates his abs. (Not that I'm looking . . .) But it's his eyes that strike me the most—the usually brilliant blue pupils are dull and sunken and shadowed. As if he's lost quite a bit of sleep. He stops short as he sees me and a look of guilt flashes over his face. But he quickly recovers and turns away, focusing instead on his Master and the Speaker.

"Is this her?" Pyrus demands, rising from the sofa and giving me a critical once-over. "Why, she's only a little girl." He walks over to me and chucks me under the chin. "Are you the big, bad monster who's got the entire Blood Coven shaking in their boots?"

"We're hardly shaking," Lucifent corrects, looking offended.

Pyrus turns on his heel, his expression full of condescension. "Well, maybe you should be," he says sweetly. "Seeing as somehow this little human girl managed to outsmart your entire organization. Got through your blood-mate program, wormed her way into your inner circle. Hell"—he gestures to Magnus, who's currently staring down at his feet as if they hold the secrets to the universe—"this one was ready to turn her into an actual vampire." He rolls his eyes. "Imagine, having a vampire slayer as a member of the Blood Coven." He laughs, as if it's the most ridiculous thing in the world. If only he knew about my sister . . .

"I'm not a slayer," I feel the need to interject. You know, since we're being honest now.

Pyrus focuses back on me, stepping forward and invading my space. He's a good-looking guy—but his breath reeks like rotten fish. I remember in the *Lost Boys* movie Rayne and I rented that bad breath was supposed to be a telltale sign of a vampire. As if his impressive set of fangs doesn't already clue me in.

"Well, then you work for Slayer Inc."

I square my jaw. "No. I don't."

SMACK! My head flies backward from the force of his sucker punch. I bite down to avoid screaming, and my mouth fills with the metallic taste of blood.

"I'll ask you one more time," Pyrus says, his jaw tightening. "And then I'll stop playing nice."

"You can ask a thousand times," I growl, hocking the mouthful of blood onto the plush carpet at my feet. The vampires immediately stiffen. I'd forgotten how sensitive they could get over even the tiniest bit of the red stuff. Better be careful or I might end up as room service. "My answer will be the same. I'm not a slayer. I don't work for Slayer Inc. I'm just a concerned party looking out for the best interests of the human race."

"Do you think I'm stupid?" Pyrus demands, looking this close to losing his cool. "You enroll in our vampire-in-training program. You seduce one of our top vampires. You attempt to win his trust by warning him about a threat to his sire's life. A threat, I'm assuming, you engineered to begin with. And then, when you think you're in, you try to talk that vampire into turning against his own people and sparking a civil war."

I grimace. I have to agree, it does sound kind of bad when you put it that way. "Hey, at least I'm not planning to unleash an army of zombies onto the world."

Lucifent's expression pales. Magnus looks up in interest. The House Speaker turns and shoots Lucifent a death look. "I thought you assured me that no one knew about Project Z," he seethes.

Lucifent squeaks, dropping his shot glass. Blood splashes on the carpet. "I swear, Lord Pyrus," he stammers, his confident swagger having completely abandoned him. "The only person who knows is General Jareth, who's overseeing the program. And I can assure you he can be trusted."

Pyrus opens his mouth to speak, but Magnus suddenly interjects. "So wait," he says. "The whole zombie thing she was talking about is true? That's really what Project Z is about?"

"I told you that you should have believed me," I mutter.

The House Speaker shakes his head wearily. "Great. Now everyone and his sire is going to know by morning."

But Magnus isn't listening to him anymore. He's turned to Lucifent, a furious expression on his face. "Why didn't you tell me?" he demands. "I'm supposed to be your second in command."

Lucifent rises to his seat. "Perhaps because I knew you'd act like this," he challenges his protégé. "What did you think we were going to do to Slayer Inc.? Ask them nicely to stop murdering us and hope they agree? They tried to kill me!" he reminds him. "They need to be punished."

"And what about the rest of what Sunny told me?" Magnus continues, this time addressing Pyrus himself. "About using the zombies to enslave the humans once Slayer Inc. was out of the way? Is that part of the plan as well?"

Lucifent frowns. "Of course not! That's ridiculous." He pauses, then turns to me. "Um, isn't it?"

"Why don't you ask your fearless leader?" I suggest.

The two vampires look at Pyrus. He releases an annoyed-sounding sigh. "Oh, don't go soft on me now," he says. "The human race has it coming to them. Why should they continue to control the world—to run the show? Face it, they're nothing more than parasites, devouring our planet like it's going out of style. One must only look at the disappearing rain forests, the melting ice caps, the fading ozone layer, global warming. Over only a few short years, humans have caused irreparable damage to the planet we share." He frowns. "But hey, why should they care? If they're lucky they might live a hundred years. Then they'll be food for worms. While we vampires are stuck inheriting the wasteland they leave behind them."

I bite my lower lip, wishing I had a response. Wishing his speech didn't actually make quite a bit of sense. I mean, I'm not suggesting zombie warfare is the answer, mind you, but I admit humans haven't really been the best caretakers of our planet.

"Eternity is a very long time to live," Pyrus adds. "And I don't want to spend mine on a postapocalyptic Hell on earth."

"I know what you're saying," Magnus tries to reason. "But

genocide isn't the answer here. We should be educating them. Using our vast resources to fund research programs that can find solutions to these problems. We should be helping the humans, rather than figuring out ways to destroy them. After all," he adds, his eyes shining with his passion, "we were all humans once ourselves."

I smile to myself, mentally cheering him on. *Go, Magnus! You tell him where it's at!*

"We *were* humans," Pyrus corrects. "But we've since evolved. And for thousands of years we've been helping others evolve, too. Artists, scientists, musicians, politicians—we've taken the cream of the human crop and turned them into vampires through our blood-mate program. Those who are left behind are useless. Except, of course, as entrées."

Ooh, he's such an ass. I squeeze my hands into fists, unable to fight down the anger welling up inside of me. "That's ridiculous," I find myself saying.

Pyrus turns to me, one eyebrow arched. "Is it?" he purrs. "But of course you would say so. Seeing as you're defending your own kind and all."

"Actually," I correct, wondering if I'm making a big mistake by bringing this up, "I'm not. I'm not a human. I'm not mortal. I'm a fairy. Princess Sunshine of the Light Court, if you must know."

Pyrus gives me a sharp look. "What?" he cries, losing his cool for a second. "But that's impossible. Where are your wings?"

"My parents left Fairyland before I was born," I inform him, trying my best to keep my voice from shaking. "They believed there was enough good in humankind to raise their children among them." I shrug. "Sure, people have made mistakes. Violence, war, destroying natural resources, *Keeping up with the Kardashians . . .*" I shudder. "But they've also done amazing things. Cured disease, built the Internet, created awe-inspiring art and music. And through it all, they've done nothing to harm the vampire race."

"Um, have you seen *Twilight*?"

I roll my eyes. "And sure, you can turn someone into a vampire once they've shown their genius. That's easy. But what about all those future geniuses that are yet to come? What if the woman you drain dry today was destined to give birth to a girl who would someday invent a way for vampires to walk in the sunlight?"

The vampires are silent, as if each is lost in his own thoughts. To my surprise, it's Lucifent who speaks first.

"Maybe this was a bad idea," he starts, his young voice full of hesitation. "I only wanted to offer up the zombies to destroy Slayer Inc. I'm not sure it's in our best interests, to be honest, to wage war with humans. In fact, some of my best friends are humans . . ."

I grin. Score one for the pint-size prince. Maybe we did do a service by saving him after all.

"Perhaps the best thing to do would be to bring this matter to the Consortium," Lucifent continues. "Let's have a real vote. See what the membership wants. After all, we are a democr—"

His words are cut off as Pyrus grabs him, rips out his throat, then throws his little body against the wall. I cringe at the sickening crack of his backbone, breaking on contact. The Blood Coven Master crumbles to the ground and remains there, still as the grave. As Magnus and I watch in horror, Pyrus casually walks up to the body, reaches down, and twists off his head.

Then he looks up at us.

"Democracy," he says, spitting out the word as if it's poison. "There will be no democracy. You are either for me or against me. This is a pinnacle moment in our history. And I can't have dissenters bringing me down." He stalks over to Magnus, his hands still dripping with blood. "What about you?" he demands. "What side are you on?"

Magnus doesn't answer at first. He's still staring at his sire's lifeless body in disbelief. Then he glances over at me—for only a millisecond. But it's enough for me to catch the regret in his eyes. He knows now he should have listened to me. Not that this knowledge does him any good.

Finally, he turns back to Pyrus, dropping to his knees in front of the Speaker. "I am, as always, your humble servant," he says meekly. "And I trust your judgment without question. If you believe the humans are worth exterminating, then I will do everything in my power to carry out your wishes."

I swallow hard, hating to watch him grovel. I know he's probably just trying to bide his time, gain Pyrus's trust while figuring out a plan to stop him. But it's still hard to see the brave and honorable vampire bowing before the evil master.

Luckily, his words seem to work. Pyrus's lips curl into a smile. He takes Magnus by the shoulders and pulls him to his feet, patting him on the back. "Well, then," he says. "I guess I should be congratulating you . . . Master of the Blood Coven."

Magnus's shoulders drop in obvious relief. Though I can see he's still shaken. I suddenly realize that we're almost back to where we were the first time around. Lucifent's dead. Magnus is Master. Pyrus is ready to kill me all over again . . .

"Thank you, m'lord," Magnus finally manages to say. "Now if you don't mind, I will take this fairy here"—gesturing to me—"and show her what the Blood Coven does to spies." He grabs me roughly by the arm and starts dragging me out of the room. I pretend to struggle, going along with the game.

"You'll never get away with this!" I cry, because that's what they always cry in movies.

We're almost to the open door—to our escape—when, without warning, it slams shut, seemingly by itself. We whirl around and see Pyrus standing directly behind us, arms crossed against his chest.

"Wait," he says in a calm, smooth voice, laced with menace.

"Y-yes?" Magnus manages to stammer. My heart starts pounding hard and fast in my chest. I don't know what he's going to say, but I can pretty much bet it's not going to be good.

"If she's telling the truth—about being a fairy—killing her would be a very big waste," Pyrus says, reaching out to pluck Magnus's hand from my arm. He wraps his own arm around me and leads me over to the couch. "Not to mention a sign of war to those in Fairyland, whom I'd very much like to have as allies." He sits me down and takes a tray of small cakes off the coffee table, offering one to me. I shake my head, disgusted.

"But . . ." Magnus stammers. "I thought . . ."

"You think too small, as usual," Pyrus rebukes him. "That's why I am the one in charge." He smirks. "Imagine, an alliance between fairies and vampire royalty. Fighting side by side, on the same team. We would be unstoppable." He smiles sweetly at me. I manage to hold back my scowl. I'd love to tell him off right now, but I know that speaking my mind may lead him to losing his temper. And I can all too clearly see the results of that, currently bleeding out on the carpet floor.

"So what are you saying?" Magnus asks, finding his tongue after a moment. "You want her to be my blood mate after all?"

"Of course not," Pyrus replies disgustedly, looking at Magnus as if he were a dim-witted child.

"Then . . . ?"

"Isn't it obvious?" The House Speaker smiles widely, revealing blinding white fangs. "I want her to be mine."

24

Rayne

"You are now free to *eat* around the cabin . . ."

The plane erupts in chaos as the queen finishes her speech. The same zombies, who up until this point have been pretty darn well behaved, considering their lack of working brain cells, start going crazy—ripping off their headphones and rising from their seats, growling and groaning and gnashing their teeth. One grabs the seat cushion in front of him, ripping it from its frame and taking a huge chomp. Bits of foam start flying everywhere. Yikes.

Guess dinner-and-a-movie time is over. Well, at least the movie part . . .

I look at Jareth. He looks back at me. Then we both turn to Glenda. "Look, Glenda," Jareth tries, though I think we both know by now it's a losing battle. "It's not what you think."

Glenda narrows her eyes. "I saw you kissing her," she reminds Jareth. "What else should I think?"

"Actually I kissed him," I interject. "And he didn't like it. At all. In fact, Jareth, you thought it was super-gross, right? And you were about to remind me that you have a girlfriend that you love very much and—"

"Silence!" Glenda commands. "Do you think I was born yesterday?"

"Glenda, darling, I can assure you I don't think that—"

Her gaze locks down on him. If looks could kill, he'd be on the floor. "You used me," she seethes. "Pretended to love me just so you could gain access to my children." She shakes her head. "Well, guess what?" she says. "You now have a full-access pass . . . to get ripped apart!"

And with that, she turns back to her impatient brood, who have gathered behind her in the doorway, struggling to be first in line for fresh meat. "Have fun, kiddos," she tells them, then ducks back into the cabin, leaving a doorway full of zombies behind her.

With vampire speed, Jareth reaches the door, attempting to slam it shut. Unfortunately, one of the zombies manages to wedge his arm in the doorway, seconds before he can lock it down. Jareth tries to bang the door against his arm, with great force, but no sense, no feeling, I guess, and the zombie keeps trying to claw his way through.

Jareth throws his full weight against the door, his face whitening with the effort it takes to keep the zombies at bay.

"I have a gun," I tell him. "But it's back in the main cabin." I glance at the door, noticing a small crack slowly snaking its way down the center. How long will it hold against the force of a dozen zombies?

"Doesn't matter," Jareth says. "We can't be using guns on an airplane anyway. If we were to shoot out a window, we'd lose cabin pressure. Then we'd all end up dead."

"No offense, dude, but that'll probably happen regardless," I remind him as I search the cabin for some kind of alternative weapon. I can hear the wood splintering behind me. We've probably got ten seconds to come up with a decent plan before they're able to bust it in.

"Um, do you guys mind if I come out now?" Spider calls from behind the door. In all the chaos, I'd totally forgotten she was in there. "I mean, I want you to have your privacy and all, but at the same time, my toes are falling asleep." She pokes her head out from the bathroom, her eyes widening as her gaze falls on the zombie arm sticking out of the main cabin door. "Uh," she says, "what did I miss?"

"Give us a hand over here," I call out, trying to drag a heavy armchair against the door.

"Looks like you already have one to spare."

"Har har. Now less banter, more battering!" I scold, pushing the chair into place. Not that it's going to do much good.

"Okay, okay." Spider reaches into her pocket and pulls out her fire stick.

"Wait!" I cry. "That's not a good—"

But I'm too late. Spider aims and fires at the zombie's arm. I squeeze my eyes shut, imaging the plane going up in a ball of flames. And us with it.

"Spider!" I cry, opening my eyes again. "Why did you . . . ?" I trail off, staring at the zombie arm. It's whitish blue and frozen in place. In fact, not just frozen in place, but literally frozen. "What the . . . ?"

Spider looks at me. "What?" she says. "You thought I was going to use fire mode?" She snorts, as if that were the most ridiculous thing in the world. "Oh ye of little faith."

"Oh *ye* of little track record."

Jareth smashes the door on the frozen arm. It shatters into a million pieces and the door slams shut. All three of us breathe a sigh of relief.

"So that thing shoots ice as well as fire?" I ask, staring at the stick in my friend's hands. It is so not fair that she scored such a powerful toy when becoming a slayer and all I got was a lousy chunk of unfinished wood. Not that I'm complaining. With her kick-ass weapon at our disposal, maybe we'll actually have a chance.

Spider frowns at the stick, banging it against her thigh. "Crap," she says. "I knew I should have charged it before we left . . ."

Or maybe not.

At that moment, three zombies crash through the door like an undead battering ram and burst into the room. There's the dapper old gent who drooled on Spider, now looking red-eyed and rabid. There's Charlie, who's growling and baring his rotten teeth in my direction. And then there's Meredith, who, well, just walked into a wall. Poor thing—it's tough to effectively maim and murder with only one eye.

I grab a bottle off the bar and slam it down on the granite countertop like I've seen people do in movies, to create a sharp weapon. It takes two tries, but I finally get it to break. Just in time for Charlie to lunge at me. I whirl around, thrusting the jagged glass at his throat. Bright green blood geysers from the wound and I leap back to avoid being sprayed. It looks pretty bad, but I guess for Charlie it's only a flesh wound, because he keeps coming, seemingly unfazed by the fact that he's hemorrhaging from his trachea.

Out of the corner of my eye I can see Spider kick her own zombie hard in the gut, grimacing at the gooshy sound her foot makes, caving into his rotting flesh. The zombie now has a combat boot–shaped hole in his abdomen, but just like Charlie, it's not slowing him down in the slightest.

"It's no use," Jareth cries over the din as he takes on Meredith. "These are no ordinary zombies!"

"Um, there's such a thing as ordinary zombies?" I ask, ducking to avoid Charlie's attack. He slams into the bar instead, shrieking in anger as he's thrown off balance.

"What I mean is these zombies aren't created by a plague or nuclear waste or some other man-made disaster like you see in the movies," Jareth explains, grabbing Meredith by the shoulders and pointing her in the direction of the bathroom. The senile old zombie stumbles inside and he closes the door behind her. Well, at least that's one down. "They've been brought back to life by Glenda—meaning she's the only one who can put them back in the ground. That's what made them so attractive to Lucifent in the first place," he adds. "They literally can't be killed."

"Oh, that's just wonderful," I mutter as Charlie finally manages to right himself and starts following me around the cabin again. I flip over a table and yank off the leg. Then I whack him as hard as I can in the head, somehow managing to spin it about 360 degrees. He stumbles and falls again. "What a great plan you guys had getting these things in the first place. Real A-plus." I suddenly notice Spider sprinting toward the main cabin door, where the rest of the undead are waiting.

"Where are you going?" I demand. "Are you crazy?"

"Are *you* a complete noob?" she asks. "I'm off to take out Glenda, of course." She turns to Jareth. "Are you cool keeping these ones out of the action?"

He nods and I realize exactly what her plan must be. And yes, I do admittedly feel like kind of a noob not to have thought of it first. I mean, hello, video game 101. Take out the boss monster and all the little creatures under her control will die, too, unable to survive without her.

Charlie grabs at my ankle, desperate for a bite. I slam my foot down on his head, crushing his skull. That ought to give me a minute or two. I jump over his writhing frame and follow Spider out to the main cabin to assess the scene.

While several zombies do appear to be milling about, others are still sitting in their seats, evidently not quite with it enough to figure out how to undo their seatbelts. Which is something, I suppose. But we've still got plenty to contend with.

Glenda stands at the far end of the plane, her face in her hands. Wait—is she crying? I feel an involuntary twinge of pity as I realize that though this woman did send an army of brain-eating zombies after me, I kind of started it by kissing her boyfriend. Or the man she thought was her boyfriend, but had been using her to gain access to her menagerie. I tried to imagine how I'd feel in the same situation. If I found Jareth kissing her and learned that he'd never loved me. I think if I had a gaggle of zombies at my disposal, I might unleash them on the guy as well.

But my feelings of pity are short-lived as a female zombie dressed in ragged Armani charges down the aisle at me. Thinking fast, I grab an overhead compartment and flip it open.

"Objects may have shifted during flight, bitch!" I cry as a heavy suitcase flies from the compartment and smacks her on the head. She falls into the row of seats to her left, colliding into another zombie. Two for one, baby. I'm on fire.

"Rayne, behind you!" Spider shouts. I whirl around to find the now one-armed door zombie stumbling down the aisle toward me, single arm outstretched and a pissed-off look on his face. I grab a seat cushion and use it as a shield as I charge in his direction, succeeding in knocking him backward into the galley kitchenette. A pot of hot coffee comes crashing down, scalding his remaining arm. He bellows in rage.

I kick him in the gut for good measure, then rejoin Spider,

who's fighting her way to the front of the plane. I watch, admiringly, as she takes out zombie after zombie, knocking each back into their rows, with only a tray table. Maybe Slayer Inc. wasn't wrong to choose her after all.

I try to follow, but it's like a game of Whac-A-Mole. She knocks them down, they get up behind her. Realizing she's now in the best position to reach the queen, I decide for the first time in my life to play sidekick instead of hero.

"Hey, uglies! Over here!" I cry, waving my arms. "Fresh brain. No waiting!"

The zombies turn in my direction and abandon Spider to start stumbling toward me instead. I back up slowly, keeping their attention. From the front of the plane I can see that Spider has reached Glenda.

"Call your creatures off," she demands, sounding fiercer than I've ever heard her sound before. "Or I won't be held responsible for what I'm about to do."

To my surprise, Glenda bursts into a fresh set of tears. "Do your worst," she sobs. "It doesn't matter anymore. My Jareth has betrayed me. What else is there to live for?"

Even from back here, I can see my friend soften. She had a bad break up with her boyfriend after he cheated on her with some chick he met during a WoW raid and is extra sensitive to the notion of guys doing their women wrong.

But we don't have time for female bonding now. The first zombie has reached me, pawing at me with filthy, clawlike hands. Behind me, One Arm has recovered and is also on the move. And I'm trapped between them. I wait for the last second, and then, as they both lunge together, I dive sideways into an empty row, forcing them to bang into one another instead, knocking heads and falling down. I'm saved for the short term but also trapped as two more zombies approach.

"Guys can be total jerks," I can hear Spider assuring our arch enemy over the din. "But you have so much going for you! I mean, you're a zombie queen—how cool is that? That alone should be worth living for."

My eyes fall upon the discarded brain on the seat in front of me. I realize, dimly, that I'm in my row. The one with my bag under the seat. I know Jareth said we shouldn't be using firearms on the plane, but at this point I'm thinking we might want to risk it. I drop to my knees, shuffling under the seat in front of me for my gun. Above me, three zombies loom, ready to pounce.

"I know," Glenda says mournfully. "It's just that I've been so lonely . . ."

Got it! I rip the weapon from my bag and dive between one zombie's legs, trying not to be grossed out by the slime. By the time he realizes where I've gone, I'm halfway down the aisle again.

"Spider!" I cry, waving the gun. "Stand back!" I stop in my tracks to aim. I can hear the zombies shuffling behind me. I don't have much time to make this shot.

"Wait!" Spider cries. To my surprise she leaps in front of Glenda.

"What are you doing?" I scream.

My friend's face takes on a determined look. One I've seen

way too many times before. When she's on a rampage, fighting for some kind of cause. "She doesn't deserve to die!" she tells me in a clear, strong voice. "The poor woman's been played. Just like everyone else."

A zombie grabs my ponytail, yanking me backward. I can feel its hot, stinky breath on my neck. Oh God.

"Spider!" I beg. The zombie opens his mouth, dragging me closer to get a good bite.

My friend turns to Glenda, giving her a beseeching look. The zombie queen sighs loudly.

"Fine, fine," she says. "But for the record, this is for you, not her." She raises her hands and claps twice, chanting something in a language I don't recognize. The zombie freezes, midchomp, then falls lifelessly to my feet. All around him the other zombies do the same. As if they've been deflated. I let out a breath of relief and collapse myself, onto a nearby seat.

"That was way too close," I mutter. I lean into the aisle to catch Glenda staring at Spider with a look of amazement on her (still tacky, I'm sorry!) face. "You saved my life," she whispers. "No one has ever done that for me before."

Spider puts an arm around the zombie queen and leads her to a nearby seat. "We girls got to stick together," she assures her. "Not let the bastards get us down."

Glenda smiles at her. "You are a good person," she says. "I would love to repay you for your kindness."

"Nah, you don't have to," Spider says modestly. "It's, like, my destiny and stuff."

"No. Your destiny would have had you kill me," Glenda

reminds her. "But you showed compassion. That's a rare thing." She purses her lips. "And so I will grant you one wish. Whatever is in my power to give, you shall have it. No matter what it may be."

Spider thinks for a moment, then glances back to me, her eyes full of mischief. I give her a bewildered shrug, having zero clue what she's trying to convey. Knowing her, it could be anything. Spider grins, then turns back to the zombie queen.

"I've got the perfect thing," she says. Leaning in close, she whispers something into Glenda's ear. I strain to catch what she's saying but can't quite get it.

But Glenda does. And she bursts out laughing. She slaps Spider on the back and rises from her seat. "Absolutely," she says, smiling at my friend. "That can absolutely be arranged."

25

Sunny

At first I think Pyrus is going to grab me and bite me—transform me into his blood mate right here, right now, no waiting. But it turns out, he's a bit more bridezilla than that, preferring Will and Kate–size nuptials rather than a down-and-dirty Vegas elopement. And all the vampire masters in town for the symposium have been invited. After all, he's got to milk this whole fairy-vampire alliance thing he's out to create for all it's worth.

Not that I should worry my pretty little head over any of it, he tells me. He'll take care of the invitations and the location, and even find me a gorgeous dress.

But that doesn't mean I get to hang out and play the slots while waiting for my big moment. After announcing his intentions, Pyrus dismisses me almost immediately, ordering his guards to lock me in a palatial-looking prison of a penthouse right on the strip. All done up in honeymoon whites and pinks and silvers, it's got a luxurious king-size canopy bed with five-hundred-thread-count Egyptian cotton sheets and gauzy, sparkling curtains. There's a pool table in one room and a massive Jacuzzi tub in another. And the full kitchen is stocked with every food I can possibly think of and some I've never even heard of. Which is nice, I suppose, seeing as after the ceremony I'll be on a blood-only diet for eternity.

Dejected, I sink down onto the velvet chaise longue, staring out onto the dazzling strip, wondering how on earth I keep ending up with guys who want to marry me against my will. At least back in Fairyland, I was under a magical spell and was oblivious to the fact that I didn't want anything to do with my future groom. Not that the clarity I'm experiencing now will help me much in my current predicament.

Half of me wonders if I should have just kept my mouth shut—not speaking up about my nonhuman ancestry. But no, then Pyrus would have just killed me on the spot. At least this way I've bought myself some time. Bought myself an eternity, actually. Though what the heck I'm going to do with it, I have no idea. Will Pyrus actually treat me like a real blood mate—allowing me to voice my opinion and rule by his side? Somehow, knowing his personality, I'm kind of doubting it.

Let's face it—I'm the trophy fairy. To be kept in an ivory tower and only trotted out during times of pomp and circumstance and political chess. Meaning I'll be living most of my eternity alone. And I'll probably never see any of my friends or

Mari Mancusi

family again. Maybe a quick death would have been preferable, now that I think about it.

The thoughts tumble around in my head, not allowing me any rest. I try to eat something—the food looks delicious—but it tastes like cardboard in my mouth. There are no clocks, so I can't tell how much time has passed, and I wonder how long he's going to keep me here before the big event. Not that I'm anxious or anything. I also wonder about my sister. Has she had better luck than me? If she can persuade Jareth to call off the zombies, well, at least that would be something. Even as a vampire, I'd much rather live out my eternity knowing the human race still exists and thrives as a dominant species.

Lastly, I wonder about Magnus. I can't help it. I know that he betrayed me—turned me over to Pyrus, of all people. I know that it's technically his fault that I'm in this whole mess to begin with. But all I can seem to focus on is the guilt I saw in his eyes as he learned that everything I told him was true. How must he feel, knowing that his disbelief led to his Master's death, not to mention my eternal damnation?

A knock on the door interrupts my reverie and my heart pounds in my chest as I tell the caller to enter. Will it be Pyrus? Or one of his flunkies, letting me know they're ready to begin the ceremony? Will I still be human come dawn?

A man dressed in a waiter's uniform walks into the room, carrying a tray of fruit. My shoulders relax. It's not Pyrus. The man closes the door behind him, sets the tray on the breakfast bar, then turns to me, pulling off his hat. I gasp as I realize it's not a waiter at all . . . but Magnus himself.

I don't know exactly how it happens, but before I know it, the two of us are tangled in one another's arms. Magnus squeezes me tight, his hands running through my hair, his lips kissing my face. I return his kisses with my own, rejoicing at the feeling of his cool skin against my mouth. This may be the last time I ever get to feel him. I'm going to make the most of it.

"Are you okay?" he asks, pulling away from our embrace and studying me with worried eyes. "They haven't . . . hurt you . . . have they?" He walks over to the door and locks it from the inside.

I shake my head, reaching out to clasp his hands in my own. "No," I assure him. "I'm fine. I mean, at least physically."

"Oh, Sunny. Oh, my love." Magnus shakes his head, dropping my hands and staring at the floor. "Can you ever forgive me? I've been such a fool. I should have listened to you. I should have believed you. You are my blood mate, after all. What I did was inexcusable." He looks up, his eyes rimmed with blood tears. "Can you ever find it in your heart to forgive me?"

I reach out to brush a smudge of blood from his cheek, gazing at him tenderly. "There's nothing to forgive," I whisper. "I'm just glad to see you, even if it's for the last time."

He pulls me close again, his breath tickling my ear as his fingers stroke my back. I allow myself to relax in his arms, living in the moment, my heart bursting with the idea that I no longer have to hide behind the lies. He knows the truth. He knows the real me. And he still loves me. Unconditionally. I try to memorize the memories we're making now—each touch, each caress. They'll be all I have to keep me warm during count-less cold nights to come.

And then he kisses me. Fully and deeply and with a des-peration that tells me volumes.

The kiss lasts forever . . . and yet ends too soon. Magnus pulls away, concern etched in his deep-blue eyes. "We have to talk," he says. And I know he's right.

He leads me over to the chaise longue and gestures for me to sit down beside him. "I've tried to get in touch with Jareth—to let him know that Lucifent is dead and Pyrus is not to be trusted. But I've gotten no answer."

I frown. "I hope nothing's happened to him and my sister. She and another slayer went to try to reason with him, just as I tried to do with you."

Magnus cringes at my words. "I hope Jareth is more open-minded than I was," he laments. "If only I had believed you, I could have prevented all of this."

"Yeah, well, I should have taken you up on the blood-mate thing from the beginning," I reply. "If I were already yours . . . and already a vampire . . . then Pyrus couldn't . . ."

I trail off, my eyes widening. I look at Magnus, wondering if he's thinking the same thing as I am. Could it work?

"No." He shakes his head. "It's a bad idea. You don't want to become a vampire, remember? You never signed up to be one. I'm not Pyrus. I'm not going to turn someone against their will."

"But I'm going to become one anyway," I argue. "If Pyrus has his way, and you know he always does." I give him a pleading look. "And trust me, if I have to become a vampire, I'd much rather be your vampire than his."

But Magnus just shakes his head a second time. "There has to be another way." He rises from the chaise longue, pacing the room. I watch as he walks over to the window and looks down. Unfortunately we're probably a hundred stories up.

"If I had my fairy wings—maybe," I say, realizing what he's thinking. "But otherwise I'm Rapunzel in this tower—with shoulder-length hair." In other words, totally helpless.

"What if we just walked out the front door?" he suggests. "You could wear my disguise and—"

Suddenly a knock sounds on the door in question. So much for that idea. We look at one another, our faces mirroring our terror. "Please, Magnus," I beg. "You've got to turn me. It's the only way to save me now."

Magnus looks away, tormented. "But he'll figure it out. And he'll kill you when he realizes you're no longer any use to him."

I shrug. "Then I'll die. It's not like I haven't been there, done that, got the T-shirt. And trust me—an eternity in Hades is a much more inviting prospect than eternal life as Pyrus's girl."

Magnus says nothing. There's another knock on the door. We're running out of time.

"Magnus!" I hiss. "If you love me—if you care about me at all—you have to do this!"

My words seem to break him from his trance. He rushes to the kitchen, grabbing a knife from a drawer. Oh thank God. "I've already taken your blood," he says as he pushes up his sleeve. "So all you have to do is drink some of mine and the bond will be complete." He slashes at his wrist with the knife and holds up his bleeding arm to me. He gives me a rueful smile. "Not exactly the romantic way I'd imagined this going down," he says.

My heart bursts as I approach him. "I love you," I tell him. "I love you so much."

I press my mouth to his wound, squeezing my eyes shut and daring to take that first suck. The one that will change me forever. I start slowly, and then, as the power of the exchange starts to consume my senses, I find myself gulping down mouthfuls of sweet blood. My mind races, mingling with his as I drink, and I can almost feel the bond solidifying between us, never to be broken apart. It's so strong and so overwhelming and so beautiful—it makes me wonder if this wasn't what was missing from our previous relationship after all.

Too soon, Magnus pulls me away. I look up at him, my eyes full of wonder, my heart bursting with adoration. "I'm yours," I whisper, reaching out to touch his cheek with my finger. "I'm forever yours."

Magnus smiles at me with such tenderness I nearly swoon. He kisses me hard on the lips. "Oh, Sunny," he whispers. "I hope you don't regret this."

I shake my head. "Never. I swear it."

A battering sound interrupts us, followed by a loud cracking as the door splinters inward. Whoever wants to get in is only seconds away.

"Duck!" I command Magnus, wiping the blood from my

mouth. "I'll get him out of here. You find my sister and Jareth. Maybe there's still a chance we can make this right!"

Magnus doesn't need a second invitation. He drops down behind the breakfast bar and I run over to the door, pulling it open before they can bust it in. I smile widely as Pyrus steps through the door, looking around suspiciously.

"Why didn't you answer my knock?" he demands. "And why is the door locked?"

I shrug. "Sorry," I say. "I was drying my hair." I reach up to fluff the hair in question, hoping he doesn't notice how unwashed it actually looks. "Wanted to look good for you when you stopped by."

He relaxes. Men are so easy sometimes. Then he smiles at me. "Everything is prepared," he tells me. "The coven masters are gathered. We will join together as blood mates tonight."

"Excellent," I say, forcing a brave smile. "I can hardly wait."

26

For someone who didn't have too long to prepare, I have to admit, Pyrus did a pretty bang-up job of setting the stage for our blood-mate nuptials. I guess it helps that they're taking place in the wedding capital of the world. Only in Vegas would you find an already decked-out Gothic wedding chapel, full of vampire kitsch and no religious icons to worry about. He even finds the perfect dress. A full-on replica of Winona Ryder's *Beetlejuice* frock. Rayne would be dying of jealousy. (Of the dress anyway. The groom, not so much.)

I glance at the grandfather clock in the chapel waiting room. Only a couple hours 'til dawn. Where is Rayne, anyway? Was Magnus able to get word to her and Jareth about what's going down tonight? And more important, were they able to stop the zombie queen from bringing her minions to town? So many unknowns. But at least I have two things to comfort me. Magnus loves me. And I will never be forced to become Pyrus's blood mate.

I wonder if Pyrus will be able to tell, when he bites me, that I already belong to another. Is there a special taste to my blood now that binds me to Magnus forever? Luckily, since Magnus already sampled my blood back in Slayer Inc. prison, there are no gaping fang holes to give my secret away. In fact, since the full transformation takes about a week, right now there's no visual way at all to tell I'm a vampire. Which buys me a little time, at least. Time for one of my sister's famous last-minute rescues, for example. After all, it's her turn, since I rescued her from Slayer Inc. back in Japan. Which now seems like a lifetime ago.

"Are you ready?" asks Trinity, the beautiful blond vampire that Pyrus assigned to help me dress. "They'd like to get started, if you are."

I reluctantly nod my assent. I'd tried to stall as much as possible while dressing to give my sister time to show up. But I'm running out of excuses and there's been so sign of her yet. I hope nothing happened to her . . .

"Sure," I say. "Let's get this thing over with."

Trinity dutifully disappears behind a red velvet curtain and a moment later reappears, just as the organ starts to play. She bows low. "It is ready," she pronounces. "Your blood mate awaits."

Here goes nothing. Forcing my feet to take one unwilling step after another, I head into the chapel. The place is packed with coven masters from around the world, seated in rows and facing a cobwebbed lectern at the other end of the room. The high ceilings are dripping in old-fashioned chandeliers, outfitted with black lights, which I guess are supposed to add to the atmosphere but actually only serve to make everyone's outfits look linty. Red candles have been scattered around the room, casting foreboding shadows on the walls, and there's even an actual coffin sitting up on a stage, decked in black roses. In other words, about as cliché Goth as you can get. Seriously, the place makes Club Fang look classy.

The organist continues to play some kind of dreadful, dismal tune as I slowly make my way down the bloodred carpet, toward the stage where Pyrus awaits. He's almost looking nervous as he stands, watching my entrance, dressed in a severe black tux, complete with red silk–lined cape. Rayne always says he looks like that singer from My Chemical Romance, but to me he resembles a young, blond Dracula. And just as scary.

Too soon, I reach the end of the road, finding myself face-to-face with the man of my nightmares. The man once responsible for issuing my death warrant, now wanting to spend eternity by my side. It's surreal, to say the least, to see him standing there, in front of me, like a Gothic bridegroom. It's all I can do to stand tall and not shake in fear.

Pyrus reaches out and takes my hands in his own. How can he do this? Bind himself to someone who wants nothing to do with him, solely to gain more power? Has he ever really been in love? Does he have any idea what it's like to give yourself to another person? Willingly sacrifice your own happiness for theirs? I almost feel bad for the guy. It must be lonely at the top. But he'll never see that. He's too consumed with greed and lust for power.

If only the other vampires in the audience could see his true colors. Know what he's planned. They could still stop him now—before he gains enough power to carry out his plans of world domination. I know there are good, decent vampires in the audience. Ones who respect the human race and would like to see it continue. But they have no idea what their leader has planned.

Maybe I need to tell them!

The thought hits me hard and fast as I realize there probably isn't a rescue on the horizon. At least not one that will come in time. And once Pyrus realizes that I've already given myself to another, it'll be game over for sure. I have a few precious minutes to speak—not to save myself—but to save the world. I have to take advantage. I may not be kick-ass like my sister, but I sure have a big mouth. And I'm more than ready to use it.

I break from Pyrus's grasp, turning to the audience and gesturing wildly for their attention. A hush falls over the crowd. The organist stops playing. From beside me, I can hear Pyrus's dismayed gasp, probably wondering what I'm about to do.

"Vampires of the Consortium!" I cry. "You must listen to me. I have something very important to tell you!"

"What are you doing?" Pyrus demands, looking at me with wild, panicked eyes. Guess he wasn't expecting me to suddenly go rogue. And now he doesn't know what to do. Sure, he could snap my neck on the spot and shut me up. But that would pretty much ruin any chance at gaining a partnership with the fairy kingdom. After all, most people aren't too keen on aligning with those who go and kill their kin. Not to mention that an act of violence out of the blue like that would definitely reveal his true colors to the rest of the Consortium, who still think of him as their nice, normal House Speaker, not a crazy insane vampire out to destroy the world.

Until I set them straight, that is.

"You have been deceived and blindsided by this man who stands before you," I continue. "You should see the things he's planning behind your backs! You think you're a democracy. But you haven't voted on any of this!"

"You idiot!" Pyrus hisses furiously. But he's drowned out by conversation coming from the audience. Pyrus turns to the assembled vampire leaders, still trying to play it cool. "You must excuse my blood mate. She's obviously under a lot of stress and—"

"Ask him about the zombies!" I cry. "Or his declaration of war against Slayer Inc. Ask him about the slayer he murdered in cold blood. Or better yet, ask him where the Blood Coven Master, Lucifent, is. I'll give you a hint. He's lying on the—"

"Silence!" Pyrus screeches, grabbing me and twisting me around so I'm flush against him. In one fluid motion, he sweeps my hair from my neck and sinks his fangs into my flesh. I can dimly hear the other vampires gasp in horror at this violent display of power. But Pyrus doesn't seem to care. He's gulping mouthfuls of my blood, pushing commands at me with all his might. Telling me to be silent, to be a good vampire, to be seen and not heard. To be his slave forever and bend my mind to his. The orders come strong and hard and fast, tidal waves of suggestion threatening to consume my brain and leave me with no thoughts of my own.

But he doesn't know my secret weapon. And my mind pushes back. My blood cells refusing to bond with his own. Namely because they've already bonded to another. And Pyrus is too late.

He rips his fangs from my neck, staring down at me with fury flashing in his eyes. "Why you . . ." he stammers. "You already . . ."

"Have a blood mate? Yes, she does."

The crowd erupts in excitement as Magnus gallantly sweeps into the room, like a knight in shining armor staging a heroic rescue. He throws me a confident grin and my heart bursts with excitement. He came. And just in time, too.

"Everything she says is true," he tells the vampires. "Pyrus has abused his power and taken advantage of our trust. He must be stopped before it's too late." He holds up his phone. "But don't take my word for it. I've just texted you all photos of his atrocities. The murder of Lucifent, Master of the Blood Coven. And the zombies he plans to use to take down Slayer Inc. and the world."

There's a shuffling as the vampires all reach for their phones at once. Thank goodness for modern technology and group text. One by one, they look up from their phones, furious as they realize the depth of their leader's deception.

But Pyrus ignores them all, looking only at Magnus. "Clever

boy," he spits out. "But none of this will save your precious blood mate." He makes a move toward me. I try to leap out of the way, but he's too fast, charging at me, hands outstretched, ready to kill me once and for all.

In a blur of my mind's eye, Magnus is suddenly standing in front of me, blocking Pyrus's reach. The Speaker slams into him full force and the two vampires tumble to the ground, growling and flashing fangs, locked in immortal combat as the rest of the Consortium looks on, frozen in place.

"You gotta help him!" I beg the audience. "He's fighting for you. For all of us!"

But just as the vampires begin to spring into action, Pyrus's guards step in, surrounding their master in a protective circle. Allowing no one to reach him. Two of them grab me—one by each arm—holding me helpless on the stage. I wonder, at first, why they don't just kill me and be done with it. But then I realize they're probably saving the honor for their master.

Pyrus takes his advantage, flipping Magnus over and pinning him to the ground. He glares down at him with ugly, red-rimmed eyes. "You could have had everything," he sneers, spit flying from his mouth as he speaks. "You could have ruled by my side. We could have taken over the world. But no. You throw it all away for some stupid girl."

"She's worth it," Magnus growls back. "She's worth everything."

My heart soars at the same time my stomach sinks. There's nothing that can stop Pyrus now. In one moment Magnus will be dead. And then it'll likely be my turn. Maybe we can meet up in Hades. See if they'll let us live together there. That would be something, at least.

As I squeeze my eyes shut, not willing to watch the death of my true love, a voice suddenly echoes through the chapel.

"What, did you start the party without us?" my sister demands.

My eyes fly open and my mouth drops as I see Rayne step through the doorway, flanked by Jareth and Spider. "Now that's just rude," she scolds.

"Especially since we brought company," Spider adds with a smug smile. She turns and gestures to someone or something behind the doorway. "Say hello to my little friends," she quips as she steps aside and lets the friends in question barrel through.

Suddenly the chapel is swarming with zombies. Disgusting, slimy, decrepit zombies. At first I start freaking out—thinking now it's really over for good. But then I realize the zombies seem to be under Spider's control somehow. And they're going after Pyrus's goons with much gusto, moaning and groaning and gnashing their teeth.

"Are you kidding me? Freaking zombies? I don't get paid enough for this," mutters one of my captors. He and his buddy drop my arms and start fleeing toward the door. The others, evidently feeling similarly about their pay grade under Pyrus's employment, join them. Spider watches them go, clapping her hands gleefully and instructing the zombies to give chase.

Now free, the vampire masters surround Pyrus, yanking him

off Magnus and dragging him away. Pyrus tries to fight back, but without his army, he's not all that tough. And he quickly realizes he's outnumbered.

"Look," he tries. "I can explain."

A vampire helps Magnus to his feet. Another leads him over to Pyrus.

"Would you like to do the honors?" she asks, holding out a wooden stake.

For a moment, I think Magnus is going to do it. He looks so fierce, so furious, as he stares with hatred at the man who murdered his sire. Who almost murdered him. Who, in another lifetime, murdered me. But then he shakes his head.

"Killing him now would make me as bad as he is," he says to the group. "Despite what he may believe, we vampires are more civilized than that. Let him stand trial for his crimes like anyone else. And let the courts decide his fate." He pauses, then adds, "We are a democracy, after all."

A cheer erupts from the crowd as two of the vampire masters lead Pyrus away—hopefully to rot in prison, until he can be officially tried. While I'm not really a huge fan of capital punishment, as a rule, in his case I can make an exception. After all, that's the only way we can be absolutely positive he can't get out and start trouble someday. Because life in prison for a vampire is a very, very long time.

Once he's gone, the Consortium members surround our little group, offering up their thanks to us for saving the day. "I feel like such an idiot," laments Thadius, the first vampire who speaks up from the crowd. "How did we not know what he was up to?"

"None of us did," Magnus assures him kindly. "We were all blinded by his smooth speech and easy lies. Well," he adds, "all of us except these two girls here, who risked their lives to tell us the truth." He shoots me an admiring look "And didn't give up, even when we didn't believe them."

The vampires nod. "We owe you a great thanks," Thadius says, addressing my sister and me. "If it weren't for you, who knows what Pyrus might have accomplished?"

I glance over at Rayne and smile. Who knows, indeed.

Before we can speak, a noise at the door interrupts. Spider bursts into the room, a huge grin on her face. "Those guards won't be troubling you any longer," she crows, rubbing her hands together in glee. "Man, it's fun to be zombie queen for a day. Too bad I have to give them back to Glenda afterward. It'd be so cool to have a gig like that permanently."

"You already have a job, remember, Miss Slayer?" Rayne reminds her with a teasing poke to her ribs. "One I have to admit you're actually pretty good at. At least when you're not setting buildings on fire."

Spider beams at the compliment. "Well, I suppose you're not so bad yourself," she replies.

A brunette vampire in a navy-blue suit turns to Spider. "Slayer, I hope you will let your bosses know that this situation has been taken care of. And there will be no war against you, at least from us. We would like to continue to live in peace and harmony from this point forward and keep you in the role of policing the otherworld for the foreseeable future."

Spider nods. "I can do that!" she declares. "I'm sure they'll be thrilled."

"We cannot allow this . . . incident . . . to harm the Consortium's image," the woman continues, turning to the other masters. "We must replace Pyrus as quickly as possible so our people do not feel any disruption."

"I agree," Magnus cuts in. "We'll hold a vote. Find the best vampire for the job."

As the others murmur their assent, I reach over to give my boyfriend a little squeeze. "Well, I know who'd get my vote," I tease.

He cocks his head in question. "And who is that?"

"You, silly," I reply. "Remember, I know the future. I've already seen your leadership abilities firsthand. And I think you'd make a very excellent House Speaker."

Yes, yes, I know. I'm the one who always complained about him working too hard. And House Speaker is probably twice the demanding job that Coven Master is. But still, I know it'll make him happy. And I know it'll help vampire kind to have a wise and benevolent ruler looking out for their best interests. So maybe I'll have to finish a movie alone or get stood up on date night once in a while—it's a sacrifice I'm willing to make.

"She's right," Jareth agrees, slapping his friend on the back. "I can't think of a better vampire for the job. You've got my vote, mate."

"And mine, too, if I can persuade a certain vampire to make

me his blood mate," Rayne adds, elbowing Jareth purposefully. He laughs, pulling her into his arms and twirling her around.

"I think that can be arranged," I hear him whisper in her ear.

"Well, that's very nice of all of you," Magnus says. "But before I can even consider a political campaign, there's something important that Sunny and I must do."

"There is?" I question. "What's that?"

"Why, reverse your vampire transformation, of course," he says, looking surprised that I haven't guessed. "I've been doing some research. If we are able to get our hands on the Holy Grail—"

I shake my head. "I don't think that'll be necessary."

Magnus crinkles his brow. "I'm pretty sure it's the only—"

"I mean I don't think I want to reverse the transformation," I say with a shy smile. "I know this may sound weird, but I'm kind of looking forward to becoming a vampire. After all, it means spending eternity by your side." I pause, giving him a loving look. "If you'll have me, that is."

"Oh, Sunny!" Magnus cries, grabbing me and burrowing his face in my neck. He squeezes me tightly, as if he never wants to let me go. "I can't think of anything I'd want more in the entire world."

And, truth be told, neither can I.

Epilogue

Sunny

And so we get our happily-ever-after. The one I used to think was reserved for storybooks. Magnus's and my relationship is better than ever, thanks to the new memories we now share. Not to mention the fact that I'm now his true partner. A vampire. A blood mate in every sense of the word. No longer worried about growing old and having him leave me behind—now we have the ability to be together forever. And he's even promised me a proper wedding, once I graduate from college. How amazing will that be?

To be honest, I don't know why I held out for so long. Being a vampire is pretty awesome, I have to admit. Sure, I don't get to go out during the day anymore, but with all I've gained from my transformation? The sun can suck it.

Pyrus is tried and convicted, and unfortunately sentenced

only to eternal life in prison, rather than the forever death. But we'll take what we can get. At least he'll never rule any sort of vampire organization ever again. The coven members have convened and chosen a new House Speaker. A leader committed to fostering a democracy, where every vampire has an equal voice.

And who scored an almost unanimous vote for the job in question? Um, yeah, that would be my boyfriend. And as his blood mate, I get a new job, too—as his coleader. I can't tell you how cool it is to stand in front of the entire Consortium and get sworn in. All those vampires who once saw me as a pathetic mortal now looking upon me with utmost respect. As we stand together, after saying our vows, we announce our commitment to continue to work toward peaceful relations with all otherworld creatures, not to mention Slayer Inc. We're even working on a treaty with the fairy kingdom, with the help of my mom and dad.

Another order of business? To reinstate all the vampires cast out of the Consortium under Pyrus's rule. Like the ones who live under the streets of New York City and fought selflessly to save Magnus and me, once upon a time. They're thrilled, of course, to be a part of the organization again and vow to serve and protect in any way possible.

It's a busy job, running a coven, and there are plenty of times, I admit, when Magnus and I collapse, exhausted at the end of the night, with no energy to do anything but sleep. But we always make an effort to take time for romance . . . to enjoy life with one another one-on-one. And our relationship is all the better because of it.

As for my sister, it doesn't take long for her to persuade Jareth to turn her into a vampire. Though not an official slayer, she continues to serve as an ambassador between the vampires and Slayer Inc., along with her friend Spider. Spider becomes the one who takes care of the werewolf cheerleaders and the evil vampires wanting to take over the world, while Rayne helps Mom and Dad defuse the threat of Apple Blossom and his fairy cohorts before our grandmother is slain. Because of this, Mom doesn't have to become fairy queen and can remain on earth and Dad can stay alive with Heather, Stormy, and Crystal. Rayne makes sure Mom still meets David, though, and, sure enough, the two of them fall in love all over again. In fact, they're planning a June wedding and have promised that Rayne and I can be bridesmaids!

In addition to her ambassador work, Rayne has also started a vampire boarding school. After her own experiences, she's realized that vampire trainees need more than a three-month course to really understand what they're getting into when they choose immortal life. So now those who want to become vampires must attend a four-year university before they're allowed to be presented with blood mates. Our half-sister, Stormy, is so excited about the new school, she's been begging her mom to let her become one of its first students.

Oh and best of all? Hades showed up to Magnus's swearing-in after party, along with Race Jameson, who ended up becoming his court musician after we left him behind. Turns out, Hades was so pleased by all the new vampire souls the zombies had provided him when taking out Pyrus's guards that he decided to trigger the bonus clause in Rayne's back-in-time contract: merging Jareth's and Magnus's current memories with those from the first time around. Now, just like Rayne and me, the boys remember both this reality and the one we effectively erased. When Jareth realized all Rayne had to go through to make his stubborn past self fall in love with her all over again, he asked her to marry him, right then and there.

So yeah, it's hard to believe, but in the end, everything has turned out for the best. Better than we could have ever imagined. And each morning, as the sun rises over the cemetery and I curl up with Magnus in our special room deep down underground in the Blood Coven crypt, I thank my lucky stars that there was a time when I dared leave normal, everyday life behind . . . to take a chance with a boy that bites.

JOIN THE BLOOD COVEN!

Do you want . . .
Eternal life?
Riches beyond your wildest dreams?
A hot Blood Mate to spend eternity with?

We're looking for a few good vampires! Do you have
what it takes to join the Blood Coven? Sign up online to
become a Vampire in Training, then master your skills at
Blood Coven University.

You'll go behind the scenes of the series, receive exclusive
Blood Coven merchandise, role-play with the other
vampires, and get a sneak peek at what's coming up next
for Sunny and Rayne.

BLOOD COVEN VAMPIRES
Check out all the Blood Coven Vampire titles!

Boys That Bite
Stake That
Girls That Growl
Bad Blood
Night School
Blood Ties
Soul Bound
Blood Forever

www.bloodcovenvampires.com

T216-0612

The Blood Coven Vampire Novels
by Mari Mancusi

Boys That Bite

Stake That

Girls That Growl

Bad Blood

Night School

Blood Ties

Soul Bound

Blood Forever

"Delightful, surprising, and engaging—
you'll get bitten and love it."
—Rachel Caine, *New York Times* bestselling author

www.bloodcovenvampires.com

penguin.com

T126-0612